BY THE GUN THEY DIED

With seven killers camped on his trail, big Blaze Morgan rides south into Weeping Woman Valley. With his superior gun skills and horsemanship, Morgan expects that he will soon shake off his pursuers. But it's a dark and a stormy night and when he's violently thrown from his horse he finds that he will be lucky to survive the next twenty-four hours ... Can he ever hope to overcome the obstacles in his way?

MATT JAMES

BY THE GUN THEY DIED

Complete and Unabridged

LINFORD
Leicester

First published in Great Britain in 2010 by
Robert Hale Limited
London

First Linford Edition
published 2011
by arrangement with
Robert Hale Limited
London

British Library CIP Data

James, Matt.
   By the gun they died. - -
(Linford western library)
1. Western stories.
2. Large type books.
I. Title II. Series
823.9′2–dc22

ISBN 978–1–4448–0735–6

Published by
F. A. Thorpe (Publishing)
Anstey, Leicestershire

Set by Words & Graphics Ltd.
Anstey, Leicestershire
Printed and bound in Great Britain by
T. J. International Ltd., Padstow, Cornwall

This book is printed on acid-free paper

1

Where Loners Ride

In the high-plains town of Jericho, Vallinova's bunch missed the man they wanted to kill by half a day.

Big Blaze Morgan had pulled out of town at daybreak, so they were told, last sighted heading in the direction of Weeping Woman Valley which nestled at the base of the mighty Flintlock Mountains.

So the seven riders swung up again on trail-stained horses and rode on out under the eyes of a town glad to see them gone.

Vallinova hadn't told them who he was or what had brought him there. There was no need. He was a too-handsome Mexican whose black garb and ornate double gunrig were ornamented with silver conchos. His back was too straight, his manner too arrogant and there was the glint of the devil in his black eyes.

'Gunfighter,' said the plain folks of Jericho, and they were right. They had made the same appraisal of the broad-shouldered Morgan half a day earlier. But not with the same note of contempt that was in their voices now. For Morgan was an American gunfighter, and that made all the difference in western Kansas where Mexicans shared a low rung on the social ladder along with redskins and nesters.

Blaze Morgan at last shook off the bunch that had been hounding him for three days solid in Weeping Woman Valley, but in doing so lost himself.

It must have happened back at the fork in the trail marked by a giant lightning-split cottonwood, the gunfighter realized as he drew up on a windy hump in the land late that afternoon. Back there at the big ruined tree there had been no telling which fork led on to the town of Mission

Fork, so he'd let a flipped coin choose his road for him.

Eyes of piercing grey played over the timbered hills and the sombre ranges shouldering the sky beyond. The trail he was following was nothing more than a faint yellow trace which twisted higher and higher into the brooding mountains. It would be a punishing climb even for a fresh man and horse, and both were far from that. Yet he knew there was no option but to keep on, for to turn back now would be to risk cutting trails with that gunfighter pack that had sworn to kill him.

So he rode on with the chill breath of the mountains in his face.

Dirty weather was building up as he pushed the appaloosa up and away from the valley. A gust of wind with flurries of snow came down off the peaks. Piled up cloud masses swirled over the stone shoulders of the mountain tops and the wind clattered like a telegraph key in the dead branches overhead.

There was dried mud on the horseman's boots and he had stubble-darkened lean cheeks. He had gone without sleep to stay ahead of the killers, and the gruelling pace was beginning to tell. His eyes felt gritty and there was a sensation of numbness in his limbs, yet he knew he must keep on. He would ignore cold, hunger, the craving for sleep and the fact that there was snow in the wind.

A humourless smile worked his lips as he eased the horse between two twisted cedars. Many claimed that gunfighting was the toughest trade in the West. He'd believed that once. But now he realized there was one thing much harder — quitting the gun trade.

Morgan frowned hard, realizing fatigue was making him light-headed. Shivering and hunching into the collar of his sheepskin jacket he felt for Bull Durham and papers in his pockets. When a man was all out of whiskey and chow there was always tobacco for comfort.

He reined in where a wooden bridge stretched across a brawling creek. The trail beyond the stream was fainter and rougher, but still climbing. The appaloosa whickered wearily, a small sound that was lost in the robust chatter and burbling of this nameless brook.

There was no need for him to roll his cigarette one-handed, but that was what he did, just to make sure his half-frozen fingers could still respond to his will. He thumbed out a brown paper, tugged the drawstring open with his teeth and sprinkled the little trough of paper full of tobacco grains, shielding it from the wind with his broad back.

Morgan then rolled the smoke with the thumb and fingers of his left hand. He licked the paper, slicked it down, twisted the end and set it between his lips, then felt in the band of his low-crowned hat for a wooden match tucked in there. He accomplished this with his right hand, the hand that could draw and fire a Colt .45 faster than just about any man in all the Kansas

Territory. He flicked the vesta into light by snapping it against his thumbnail.

The quick spurt of match flame highlighted the sun-bronzed face, the intensity of the grey eyes, the tiny sun-wrinkles at their corners and the thin scar that traced its course down to the point of the jaw.

Though deeply etched with weariness this was still a formidable face, by any standard. Challenging. Seeing Blaze Morgan, people would instinctively feel respect and avoid looking for trouble.

Men had stepped aside for him in Jericho, Mulligan's Flat, Tumbleweed and in all those one-horse hell towns where men with mouths greater than their gunskill had gone crashing down under the authoritative bellow of the youthful Blaze Morgan's Navy Colt . . . back in the times when he'd gone looking for danger, not attempting to avoid it as was mostly the case now.

The rider shook himself from his reverie as he approached the creek. Thunder continued to growl and mutter over the hunched and mighty shoulders of the Flintlocks. Now thunderheads were massing. From a distance, the rain resembled a smoking, drifting fabric of some kind hanging from the underbelly of the clouds, moving slowly from south and east, angling towards him, turning swiftly in the driving sleet.

The first fat drops hit and burst against the bridge, stippling the swirling waters. There must be heavy rain high weather coming — he suddenly found himself imagining sturdy ranch houses, cherry-red fires, warm, clean blankets . . .

With a mutter of impatience he flipped the cigarette stub aside and started for the bridge. The tobacco had helped ease the grinding hunger in his belly, but how long could he keep going on nicotine and smoke?

Ancient bridge timbers creaked and groaned alarmingly beneath horse and rider as they crossed, and Morgan touched the animal's flanks with spurs the moment the crossing was behind them, eyes stabbing left and right. This trail had to lead *somewhere*.

Within an hour, maybe two, he was losing track of time, and the rain-lashed night gradually grew as black as the inside of a preacherman's hat.

Morgan was by this time too dulled by exhaustion and too unfamiliar with the region to be aware that he was now travelling through a high mountain valley which was almost as level as the ranchland he'd left four thousand feet below outside Jericho.

Next instant a bolt of lightning ripped through the dark skies, striking — or so it seemed — almost on top of man and beast. The horse squealed, reared, lost its footing and toppled. Morgan struck ground with sickening force, yet instinctively rolled away from the animal's tumbling body. As the darkness enveloped him again, darker than it had been before, he started shouting for the animal only to hear frantic hoofbeats receding in the blackness.

He started to stumble onwards, would never know how far he travelled thus that evil night. He only ever remembered rain, cold and exhaustion combining in an effort to bring him down, yet always failing, through a night without time — until suddenly came the shock of both knees striking the earth simultanously.

He was down and knew he would never have the strength to rise. The sleet-filled winds buffeted him relentlessly and his breath was ragged and weak in his throat.

Strange . . . but he never figured the end might come like this . . . without a few last words . . . without seeing Grace just one last time. He'd always figured dying would be different from this — maybe going down in some muddy front street with his body full of bullets and the thunderclap of raging Colts his last sound on earth — not dying alone in the rain and the cold before a great mansion in the mountains . . .

That final dim thought had come and

almost gone before Morgan grasped its significance.

Slowly his streaming head came up.

Mansion . . . ?

A burst of sheet lightning illuminated the entire landscape — and there it was. Three storeys high, gabled and tiled, encircled by deep galleries ornamented by lacy ironwork, with darkened windows staring down at him like blind eyes. It loomed above his kneeling figure, reminding him of those great plantations that once seen were never forgotten in the Deep South which he'd ridden from the sea to Atlanta with Sherman's all-conquering armies long ago.

He clenched his eyes shut and counted to twenty before looking again. The world was now darker than a pawnbroker's soul and he was about to curse the gods for toying with him so cruelly when the lightning hissed and shimmered brilliantly again, and when he reached out desperately to seize the elaborately carved gallery railing he found it to be real.

Clutching the solid timber with both hands, the exhausted Morgan groaned aloud. Yet when he attempted at length to draw himself erect, he found he was able to make it. He stood for a long minute, swaying. Another step, and he was able to hear the wind moaning in the eaves, and somewhere out back, a shutter clattered.

With new vigour, he grabbed at the railing and began hauling himself up. He counted the steps. Five of them. And then suddenly the sleet was stinging his face no longer and he realized he was standing on a wide gallery and there was a solid roof above his head.

Blaze Morgan felt life rushing back into his limbs, painful but thrilling. He swung his arms to bring the circulation back. At that heady moment there was but the one characteristic thought: Blaze Morgan was not finished after all.

Feeling his way along the mansion wall towards the front door, Morgan passed a recessed window. The heavy, dark drapes were tightly drawn, yet he glimpsed a faint sliver of yellow light, and reasoned that the place was occupied. So he banged hard fists on the wall and hollered, 'Hello, the house!'

No response.

He waited several seconds before he started shouting and kicking again. OK, he'd revived some but was still in no shape to be left out in the wind and cold of a miserable night. His energy didn't last long. He leaned a moment against the wall, reckoning now that the reason he'd had no response was that it would be hard hearing anything above the roar of the storm.

So he felt his way along the wall again and came to the door. He cocked a fist then beat on the timber before sighting the big metal knocker. He raised it then slammed it down — hard.

Still nothing. So he continued banging and kicking until realizing all he was achieving was burning what little juice he had left now.

He pulled his six-shooter, stepped back a pace then blasted the lock into trash with a roar that drowned out the voice of the storm.

He poked the door with the smoking gun muzzle and it opened silently to reaveal a big gloomy hallway with three doors opening off it. Further along, a heavy staircase led up to the floor above that was lost in darkness. There was no lamp in the hall, the only faint illumination coming from a doorway to the left.

'Hello!' he yelled, and closed the door behind him.

He waited. Nothing happened. He was getting to feel chilled and weak again. Taking a fresh grip on his gun butt he started off for the tall narrow chink of doorlight. He didn't call, didn't muffle his steps. If there was anybody home they'd have heard him by this. Strange nobody had responded to all the racket . . .

He shoved the door open with the

13

muzzle of his six-shooter, paused a moment then crossed the threshold.

The room was large and gloomy and roughly furnished. There was a battered old table directly beneath a sputtering drop-light, with three battered chairs set around it. A bulging sofa with busted springs, a potbellied stove bedded upon a square of tin. On one side was a big box serving as a wood-bin, on the other a doorway standing open to reveal a narrow hallway.

His attention quickly returned to the table and its one greasy plate upon which rested a half-eaten haunch of venison.

He didn't hesitate now.

Three long strides and he'd snatched up the haunch and torn into it with the ferocity of a starving man.

Sixty seconds was roughly the time it took for a half-haunch of venison to be reduced to one bare bone, which was tossed aside as Morgan flexed his wide shoulders, inhaled deeply and knew he'd defeated the Old Man With The Scythe — again.

He scouted around the floor for some time without coming across anything significant — and still no sign of occupants. So he grabbed the light and set off to explore with one hand on his belted gun — just in case.

He eventually climbed to the first floor which proved a grey, uninspiring replica of the ground level until he came to an outsized room that was lavishly decorated with elaborate furnishings and thick carpeting.

Morgan had seen places like this during the War Between The States, great handsome homes of the southern cotton kings, most of them stripped bare by their once affluent owners when the Yankees were coming through on their final, great triumphal march.

But that was in the once rich South where so many were rich. This was some lofty ranch house set high and away from anything resembling civilization in the wild and snowy mountains.

How come?

He quit the room and began prowling again but found little of further interest other than one small room which appeared better cared for than the others, and where he was sure he detected a faint whiff of scent . . . woman's perfume?

Or was he so beat that he was imagining things?

He entered the room adjacent, sighted a gloomy old bed, threw himself upon it and was instantly drowsy. So the loner slept — unaware his Colt was still clenched in his fist as if instinct was telling him he might need it . . .

2

Ranchero Sinister

The ceiling above their heads creaked and shuddered under the impact of the storm and specks of plaster floated down, but neither Morgan nor the youth with the shotgun noticed.

He was indeed only a youth, a sleep-heavy Morgan realized in that jarring moment of awakening. Around seventeen would be his guess, with a pale thin face framed by golden blond hair. And a shotgun in his hands.

He started next moment when he saw that young face seemingly duplicate itself. Morgan shook his tousled head, wondering if this could still be part of the dream he'd been having, until finally sleep-dulled senses realized that a girl with the face of an angel had moved up beside the youth

17

to take him by the arm.

Gravely, silently, the couple gazed down upon him in unblinking silence as though only waiting for some sign or signal to blast his wildly thudding heart clear out of his ribcage.

He pushed his back up against the rungs of the bed head, struggling to find his voice. He still felt drugged by lack of sleep and exhaustion, was slow to recover full alertness while acutely aware he must.

It seemed an eternity before he realized it was daylight with the dull grey of morning sheening the windows. The lamp had burned itself out and, though that wind still moaned, the night's sleet had gone.

'Now?'

It was the boy who spoke and he was asking the question of the girl. She appeared uncertain with her enormous eyes fixed upon Morgan's unshaven face, until he saw her compress her lips and the golden head nodded.

'Now, Lukey!'

Morgan worked saliva into his mouth and swallowed. The back of his shirt was drenched with sweat by this. He could feel chilly rivulets coursing down his flanks. It seemed plain he was but a hair's breadth away from death, but then all his danger-honed senses were clearing and his iron nerve was kicking in.

And only with full alertness came the realization that the shotgun and the hands holding it were extended out over his boots!

Morgan kicked upwards violently just as the youth squeezed trigger. There was a roar like a plug of dynamite going off in a confined space and a gaping hole immediately appeared in the ceiling as the gun was knocked upwards.

The girl screamed as the gunfighter hurled blankets aside and threw himself at the youth who was staggering back from the bed, trying to steady himself for another shot.

The brass bed-end buckled as Morgan's hurtling body weight crashed down upon it, but he didn't even feel the pain. His entire being was concentrated only upon that gun, and now his right hand was wrapping around the hot barrels and thusting them ceilingward.

Again the shotgun erupted with a great bellow that reverberated insanely in that confined space and a shower of ceiling plaster came raining down upon all three.

Morgan's power and momentum saw him drive the youth before him into a crashing fall at the base of the wall, the girl spinning heavily to the floor from a glancing blow from his leg.

The boy's head struck the wall as Morgan's fist slammed his jaw. He dropped like a stone. Rolling across the unconscious figure, Morgan heaved himself into an upright seated position against the wall to see the girl clawing for the Colt that had been knocked from her grasp in the scuffle.

'Judas Priest!' he snarled and, plunging his hand into his pants top, brought it up instantly filled with derringer. His lips were drawn back in an animal snarl as he roared, 'Freeze, girl! Touch that and you're dead!'

It was a chillingly effective warning delivered by a man capable of backing up his words with action. Or was he? For only in that breathless moment was Morgan fully realizing just what a slender wisp of a young woman she really was. She didn't appear old enough to quit school, much less be playing games of life or death with a man who could, if he chose, carve notches in the handle of his gun.

For a hanging moment, Morgan really thought she was going to grab the gun anyway and he would have to kill her. But in an instant she was crawling swiftly away on her knees to the supine figure on the floor. 'Oh, Lukey, Lukey! What did he do to you?'

'He's all right,' Morgan heard himself declare gruffly. His ears were still ringing from the two mind-deadening blasts of the shotgun, his vision hampered by the twists of gunsmoke that still clouded the room.

He cleared his throat and squared his shoulders. 'You can relax. I just clipped the young fool, which is a damn sight better than he deserves.'

The young woman gave no sign she'd heard as she cradled the unconscious boy's head in her lap, tenderly stroking the darkening bruise on his jaw where Morgan's fist had crashed home.

'Lukey!' Her voice was thin and fearful, almost childlike. 'Lukey, please say something.'

Shaking his head to clear it, Morgan got up and scooped up the shotgun. It was a Richardson, a brute of a weapon. Like all shotguns, it was next to useless at any range other than up close, when it could kill a bull buffalo with one barrel. It was not a weapon you'd expect to find in the hands of kids. But then, maybe these were anything but an everyday breed of kids?

'Will you shut that blubbering?' he demanded roughly, flipping the empty shotgun onto the bed. 'Just count yourself lucky the fool isn't damn-well dead!'

Before, he'd acted instinctively, but now he was angry.

'What the hell is all this about anyway?' he wanted to know 'Who are you? And what's the big idea of trying to shoot a man in his bed?'

His words were wasted. The girl's entire attention continued to be focused on the youth. Then there were more tears. Scowling hard, Morgan sucked his knuckles and wondered if maybe he had punched a little too hard. He was relieved when the boy's eyelids began to flicker and, with relief, the anger returned.

He took down his gun belt and buckled it around his middle, feeling for the first time the after-effects of crashing upon that bed-end. As he hauled on his boots the youth opened his eyes, stared about vacantly for a moment then turned to the girl.

'Hannah?' he said vaguely.

'It's all right, Lukey,' she told him, smiling at last.

'Everything is just fine and dandy,' growled Morgan, hefting the weapon again. 'You damn near killed a man who never did you one lick of harm, and you've shot up a fine room all to hell . . . and could both be dead right now. But, even so, everything's just peachy.'

The boy hauled himself up into a seated position and, with the last dregs of unconsciousness clearing from his eyes, stared up at Morgan with an expression that seemed peculiarly devoid of any emotion. And now that her tears were drying up, the girl's face was also slipping into a replica of the brother's blank expression.

Neither spoke. They looked as if they might mean to sit there in silence until doomsday. That didn't suit Morgan. He had come close to death and meant to find out who had tried to kill him and why. He gestured at the boy with the empty Richardson. 'What's the rest of your name?'

'Garfield.'

'Luke and Hannah Garfield?' he guessed.

Both nodded. They were very alike, each slimly built, the boy with shoulders that would be strong one day, the girl's lithe lines just beginning to bud into womanhood. But what mainly caused Hannah and Luke Garfield to look more like twins than brother and sister with just a couple of years between them, was their common facial expression. It was an odd mixture of fear, defiance, apathy and something else the gunfighter couldn't identify, yet which caused him a strange feeling of unease.

He motioned them to their feet with the shotgun. When they complied, he tossed the heavy Richardson onto the bed.

'All right,' he said, slipping his hands flat behind his belt and squaring his shoulders. 'Let's hear it.'

Blank stares were his response. Morgan's features settled into harder lines.

'I'm not fooling!' he rapped. 'I want to know where your folks are and how come you tried to kill a man you'd never even seen before.' He jabbed his finger almost in the boy's face. 'And I mean to know now — bucko!'

The girl made a small sound of protest, but fell quiet when the boy touched her arm.

'It's all right, Hannah,' he sighed. 'He has the right to an answer, I guess.'

'Damn right I have!' Morgan affirmed.

'We heard you come in during the night,' Luke Garfield stated and, watching intently, Morgan was beginning to see a pattern of behaviour emerging. When speaking to one another, the boy and girl sounded quite normal. It was only when addressing him they adopted that dead monotone, which the boy employed now as he went on. 'We were scared and we hid. We thought you were an outlaw. We feared you might harm us when you woke up, so we decided we had to kill you first.'

'And that's it?' Morgan challenged,

dark brows arching upwards. 'Is that what you'd have put on my marker? 'Morgan — shot in mistake for an outlaw?'

'Your name is Morgan?' Luke asked.

'Blaze Morgan.'

'I'm sorry, Mr Morgan.'

'You don't damn well sound it.'

The youth shrugged and dropped his gaze, leaving Morgan feeling as if a curtain had just come down.

'Where are your folks?' he demanded.

'We live here alone,' answered the girl.

'No folks?'

Two heads shook and Morgan's hard features seemed to soften a little. 'Just where is here, anyway?' was his next query.

'Atlanta Ranch.'

'Uh-huh,' Morgan grunted, heading for the window. 'And . . . who built this crazy big house?'

'It was left us by our grandmother,' the boy said tonelessly. 'She's dead also.'

Morgan rolled a smoke one-handed as he gazed out the window.

He could see clearly now what he hadn't been able to last night. The house was situated in the centre of a beautiful valley encircled by towering cliffs which lifted in rugged battlements in the grey morning. A restless wind whipped across the landscape, stirring the deep grasses like the waves of the sea.

Everything was strange, he mused. And yet oddly everything about this place, including his journey to reach it, seemed to fit together somehow.

First there had been that lonesome trace of trail which had led him to a ranch where you'd never expect to find one; the great house seemed as improbable as the ranch itself, and yet somehow this boy and girl appeared and acted just strangely enough to appear to suit their surroundings.

Last night much of the strangeness he'd encountered might have been attributable to his exhausted condition, further heightened by the storm. Yet even in broad daylight he had to concede that Atlanta Ranch and its youthful occupants appeared to be just a tad unnerving and on the strange side.

Smoke trickled from his lips as he stared from one to the other with level grey eyes. 'How long have you been here?' he asked finally.

'A long time,' replied the boy.

'And just how long is that?'

'A long time,' Hannah Garfield repeated, and met his stare unflinchingly.

'So, that's how it's to be, is it?' Morgan growled. 'All right, I'll ask just one more question. Where's the nearest town with a sheriff?'

That struck home. He saw them pale, heard the catch in the boy's voice when he replied, 'A sheriff? You mean . . . for us?'

'You must have been up here too long,' Morgan said harshly. 'People still swing or go to jail for murder down there below in the real world.'

The pair slipped arms about each other at that and the girl began weeping, burying her face in her brother's shoulder. Morgan held his hard stare for as long as he could, yet felt a stirring of sympathy. There was no denying they'd attempted to kill him, but that didn't alter the fact they were still only kids. Vulnerable kids it would seem at that moment.

And who could tell what they might have been through, he grudgingly mused following a long silence? Living up here alone in an eerie old mansion cut off from the world? Maybe their reason for trying to kill him had been simple self-preservation after all. It was possible, he supposed.

'All right, damnit!' he said roughly. 'Maybe I won't go running to the John Laws — yet. I'm still peeved . . . but maybe I might let bygones be bygones . . . say, for a plate of ham and eggs?'

They stared at him suspiciously, then drew away a little to confer in whispers.

At length the boy turned back. 'You'll really go if — ?'

'I said I would. I always keep my word.'

He sounded convincing; he convinced them.

'I'll go fix the meal,' Hannah said. 'Lukey can help you look for your horse.'

'I give the orders around here,' Morgan growled, hefting the shotgun and slinging it across his shoulder. 'You help your sister fix the grub, boy, and if I find my horse you can give him a feed and rubdown.' He dry-clicked the triggers of the shotgun. 'And just in case you've got any more weapons about the place, just leave 'em lie. Better men than you have been trying to kill me for years, and all they got for their pains was the Deep Six. You compre . . . Junior?'

Luke Garfield was pale yet had grit enough to speak up. 'Then you are a gunfighter, right?'

'Ham and eggs, sunny side up,'

Morgan grunted and walked out, turning his back on them. As he descended the stairs he listened to the echoes of his steps coming back at him from empty rooms and hollow chambers, heard the eerie creaking of old timbers all around.

Outside he encountered a big old hound with mournful eyes moving about the outbuildings. With the shotgun slung over his shoulder he started off through the grass which grew long right up to the mansion walls. He made a vague guess at the route he had followed last night and struck off in that direction.

He refused to glance back until he'd covered a couple of hundred yards. The house still appeared mighty strange, standing up there in its sea of grass, so he thought, yet was now maybe a tad less spooky and alien-seeming than when he'd seen it first in the deep of night.

He glanced up and sighted the Garfields. They stood side by side in a big bay window on the first floor, not moving or speaking, just staring out at him with eyes fixed and unblinking.

Morgan felt himself shiver slightly as he turned his broad back and knew it wasn't from the cold.

* * *

A pallid yellow sun was struggling to fight its way clear of the clouds an hour later when Morgan reappeared from the north-west to come striding back towards the Atlanta headquarters.

He carried a saddle and bedroll slung over his shoulder and had the appaloosa's reins looped through his arm. He'd found his horse without much trouble about two miles from the mansion. The animal was still played out from the previous day's hard ride, but otherwise was in good shape.

The appaloosa nickered a greeting to the ranch horses in the corral as Blaze led it into the yard. The horses responded but the Atlanta's ancient plough mule wheeled and raced off to the far side of the corral. There it stood snorting and pawing at the ground, glaring wildly at both Morgan and his horse as though they were a pair of mule-eating lions down from the high country.

Grinning at the animal's performance, Morgan led his mount into the gloom of the stables and had set to work with brush and curry comb when Luke Garfield walked in.

'The food is ready,' the youth said and held out his hands for the grooming implements.

Morgan passed them over wordlessly and was making for the doors when he glimpsed the saddle on the tree. It was a big double-girthed Texas Spanish saddle with wooden stirrups that hung low. He paused to study the rig a moment before turning to see Luke already at work.

'This your saddle, boy?' he asked.

The blond head nodded but Luke didn't look up.

'Must be risky, riding a boss without being able to reach the stirrups,' Morgan remarked, flapping the leathers with his fingers. 'This here is a tall man's saddle, sonny.'

'Sis said to tell you your breakfast is getting cold.'

A scowling Morgan swung on his heel and strode out into the restless wind.

What did he care if they lied to him? He had more things to occupy his thinking time than a couple of kids who seemed bent on playing some spooky game that likely scared themselves more than it did anybody else.

Things, such as making sure he kept well ahead of one Juan Vallinova, the notorious Mexican pistoleer and lethal brother to the late Miguel Vallinova, who now slept the long sleep in a tiny boot hill outside the Oklahoma border town of Yellow Gulch — with Morgan's bullets still in him.

A consideration like that was guaranteed to keep boredom at bay, even for a man who sat as tall in the saddle as Blaze Morgan.

There was no sign of the girl as he entered the house, but his sense of smell led him to the big front room with the rusted old stove. A huge plate of ham and eggs was on the table with a coffee pot standing within easy reach. Both food and coffee were piping hot from the stove, but there was no sign of any cook.

With a shrug Morgan took his place at the table and started on the food with a will, washing it down with cups of hot coffee liberally laced with sugar. Yet hungry as he was he soon found himself merely picking at the second half of his breakfast, his thoughts once more diverted by his hosts.

By nature Morgan wasn't a man to intrude on another's privacy, yet by the same token he wasn't able to overlook any situation which simply failed to ring true. Such things honed his senses sharp and his refusal to ignore such warning signals had saved his life more than once.

There was enough that was odd

about Atlanta Ranch to intrigue most anybody, he reflected, as he stirred sorghum into his second mug of good joe.

The strangeness of the great house situated in such a remote and inaccessible place intrigued, while it seemed obvious that a couple of kids wouldn't be capable of running such a place for any length of time.

He'd glimpsed lumber stacked in the back of the stables such as only a strong man could have handled. Then there was that saddle with the long stirrup leathers, plus the fact that he'd seen two other fully furnished bedrooms beside the two the brother and sister occupied. Even that big old chair over in the far corner had plainly been designed for someone much larger than Luke Garfield.

So . . . who else lived here in the high valley? And why had Luke and Hannah lied to him after failing to kill him or scare him off?

He was still brooding over coffee and

a cigarette a short time later when a sound from out back attracted his attention.

He realized that it was the mournful howling of a dog.

Quitting the room he passed along the short, gloomy passageway which led to the back porch. From there he looked out over a cluster of sturdy outbuildings comprising stables, barn, tack-room, meat house and smithy. He could not see the dog but the sounds appeared to be emanating from the smithy.

Morgan massaged the back of his neck. Although he kept telling himself he wasn't really over-interested in either this house or its occupants, things seemed to keep popping up to stir his curiosity. That dog, for instance. Dogs never howled that way in daylight unless they were lonely or something was wrong. So what was ailing that flea-bag?

He was about to go investigate when he felt rather than heard somebody behind him. Whirling, he dropped hand to gun butt. The girl stood framed in the doorway, holding his sheepskin jacket. He saw at a glance the garment had been cleaned and dried. He ventured a grin but it wasn't returned. So he jerked a thumb over his shoulder and said, 'I was just wondering what's ailing your dog.'

'It howls all the time,' she replied. 'Here's your jacket, Mr Morgan.'

'Here's your hat — what's your hurry?' he said sharply, taking the sheepskin. 'All right, little lady, you don't have to beat me over the head for me to know I'm not welcome. The bed and grub were just fine but the hospitality is lousy. I only hope that whatever weird game you and your brother are playing here doesn't blow up in your faces, which seemes likely sooner or later . . . '

He flipped his hat and caught it.

'To put it plain, Miss Hannah, the next geezer to get lost in a storm up here just might talk a whole heap less and shoot a sight quicker than I do. I hope you remember that for your own good. Having said that, I'll say what you've just been busting to hear all along. Adios.'

She didn't reply. He would be surpised if she had. She merely stood there watching him turn towards the passageway, a child with an old woman's reserve about her . . . maybe a child like the one he might have had himself had not the war and the gunfighting years intervened . . .

That thought brought a bitter taste to the big man's mouth as he crossed the front room. He was reaching for the doorknob when he suddenly picked up the sound of hoofbeats.

'Vallinova!' he guessed, and his right hand went streaking for gun butt.

3

Of Blood and Grass

His right hand was filled with six-shooter as he lunged for the window. The drapes were only partially drawn and through the gap he saw two men astride big horses moving slowly and deliberately in past the corrals.

A glance was all Morgan required to know he'd never seen either man before. But that was hardly reassuring, for he didn't know how many men Vallinova — the killer who hunted him — might have riding with him. What he did know was that both these strangers had the reek of trouble about them which some men got to wear like a second skin over time.

The two drew rein at the corrals, hard eyes flicking this way and that, hands resting on gun handles now. As

Morgan glimpsed Luke Garfield emerge from the stables leading his saddled appaloosa, he heard a faint sound behind and swung to see the girl standing in the hall doorway.

She drew her eyes away from his crouched figure as if it were an effort, then crossed to an adjacent window to gaze out. Her golden head shook in response to his questioning stare. 'I don't know who they are,' she stated.

'Likely lying again,' Morgan snarled, and when she turned to face him, added, 'You say you don't know them, but if that's so, why are you scared half out of your wits? Judas! I mortally hate a liar . . . '

His voice trailed off as his attention was drawn back to the scene outside. The girl's stare remained fixed upon him. Her lips were dry. Morgan had been right when he'd figured Hannah Garfield was afraid, but he hadn't pinpointed the real reason for this as yet. For it seemed less those two strangers who scared the girl, than the manner in which Morgan had whipped out that big gun of his so murderously fast in a way that reminded her chillingly of the one man she had hated and feared all her unhappy life.

★   ★   ★

Saddle leather creaked as Billy Jake Foley turned this way and that, bright brown eyes taking everything in. The curly-headed badman was trying to appear unimpressed, yet clearly was. Poverty born and bred and a longtime rider of the owlhoot trails, young Billy Jake had never seen a house such as this in his life.

Idly fingering the bone handle of his Peacemaker Colt close by, Aaron Carney was no less startled by what they had stumbled upon up here in the high Flintlocks, but made a better fist of concealing his feelings. Long and lean, with saturnine features and ice-pick eyes, Carney was wanted in two states for murder and another for train robbery. A man didn't rack up that kind of a record without developing a good poker face to go with it.

The outlaws finally turned their backs on the mansion when a soft plodding of hooves warned that Luke Garfield was emerging from the stables. The boy was leading Blaze Morgan's big spotted horse.

'Hold it right there, pilgrim!' ordered Foley, the gabby one of the pair. Luke duly halted and Foley fingered his hat back from his forehead to loose a tumble of curls so black they appeared to have been laundered in coal-oil. Foley put on a mean look. 'Who be you?' he challenged.

Luke surveyed the pair gravely, only shaking hands betraying his nervousness. 'I'm Luke Garfield,' he stated. 'What do you want?'

'Chip said Jesse had a couple of young 'uns up here, Aaron,' Billy Jake muttered to his partner.

'Yeah, so he did,' drawled Carney in a voice that was pure Texas. His maverick eyes cut to the youth. 'So, where's your pa, boy? Me and Billy Jake here are good pards of his.'

'Good pards,' lied Billy Jake, puffing up his chest.

'Pa ain't here.'

'So, where is he, then?' Billy Jake wanted to know.

'Don't know. He just up and left.'

Carney's mean eyes narrowed. 'So . . . just when did he go, kid?'

Luke lowered his gaze. 'I don't rightly recall. I don't remember much about anything.'

Billy Jake nodded to Carney. 'Chip also figured there was somethin' spooky about the Garfield whelps. This one don't look none too bright to me.'

'Mebbe, mebbe not,' Carney answered. Then suddenly his voice cracked sharper. 'Lift up your fool head and listen to me, boy. I'm lookin' for your pa and another pard of mine by the name of Chip Greenberry. Now I got a right strong hunch that mebbe they are both up here someplace and it'd be right smart if you'd tell me just where.'

But Luke refused to lift his head. 'Don't recall,' he muttered again. Then let the horse's reins drop and started for the house.

A touch of steel sent Billy Jack's flashy black jumping forward to cut him off. Luke stared up at the cocky hardcase with fear showing plainly in his eyes. He made to back up but Carney's high-shouldered buckskin had moved in behind him.

Carney deliberately drew his Colt .45 and held it resting upon his thigh.

'Now, get this, kid,' he drawled, 'me and Billy Jake didn't come hoo-rawin' up here to mess with any half-growed sprout. But if you don't come clean in a big hurry about our pard Greenberry and your old man you're goin' to end up one sick and sorry yearlin', and that's the simple truth.'

'And you'll be wearin' your hat back to front too,' added Billy Jake. He leaned from his saddle and smiled crookedly. 'Now, where are them beauties — them and all that big dinero?'

There was silence for a long moment, before Carney suddenly yelled, 'By Glory! Did you see the way his eyes turned when you mentioned the dough? This runt does know all about it — sticks out a mile!'

Luke desperately attempted to run. He didn't get far. Heeling his horse forwards with spur, Carney expertly knocked the boy clear off his feet with a bump from the buckskin's barrel chest. He lay dazed for a moment and by the time his head cleared the lean Texan had swung to ground and was now advancing with six-gun in fist and brutal intent in his eye.

Carney was reaching out for Luke when a sharp cry sounded from the house. The hardcase swivelled, six-gun at the ready as his eyes stabbed at the windows.

'Sounded like a gal, Aaron!' Billy Jake panted, brandishing his gun. 'Likely the sister.'

'Go take a look,' Carney barked, seizing a handful of Lukey's shirtfront. He placed the muzzle of the weapon against the boy's temple and filled his lungs to shout. 'Listen good, you in the house. One wrong move and this here tad gets his brains spattered.' He jerked his chin at Foley. 'Get in there smart and see to the dame!'

Foley hesitated. He was a gritty hardcase but held a deep respect for his leader, the missing Chip Greenberry. He didn't care to go busting into that big house in case Greenberry was inside and hostile. But before he could voice a protest, the Texan's voice sounded again.

'Do like I say, you curly-headed son of a bitch! Garfield ain't goin' to try nothin' while I got a gun on the kid, and he ain't about to let Chip try nothin' neither. Now hustle and see if we can flush 'em.'

This made sense to Billy Jake. And it was with a cocky grin to show he wasn't worried one lick, that he raised his Colt and booted his mount for the house . . . directly towards the yawning mouth of Blaze Morgan's Navy Colt.

★ ★ ★

The disdain the girl felt for Morgan lasted no longer than the time it took the lean flanked Carney to knock her brother down with his horse. In an instant she was across the room to Morgan's deeply recessed window where she shook his shoulder violently and insisted he start shooting while her brother was still breathing.

Morgan brushed her aside. He didn't take his gaze from the drama being enacted out there in the wind as he spoke. 'Who are these men?'

'I don't know. But it's plain they are evil and mean Lukey harm. Oh, please do something, Mr Morgan . . . '

Before Morgan could react the taller horseman swung to ground and started for the dazed Luke, gun in hand. This brought a scream from the girl at

Morgan's side and he cursed under his breath when he saw both men turn and stare sharply towards the house.

Suddenly the taller hardcase seized hold of the boy and bawled a warning. Morgan was gripped by indecision. Were they scouts for the hellion, Vallinova, or merely just a pair of hardnoses bent on some private hell-raising of their own?

There was no telling. And now the girl was pulling at his shoulder again.

'Please, Mr Morgan. You must do something!'

There was nothing new about this situation for Blaze Morgan. Ever since cutting down his first badman in Texas there had been somebody in the next town, around the next corner or even someone maybe wearing a skirt — with the kind of big problems only his six-gun seemed able to handle.

And the cry was always the same: 'Please, Mr Morgan . . . Please help!'

Yet most always, after the gunsmoke had blown away, human nature being what it was, they were ashamed of being forced to plead and beg . . . and most would rather cross the street than have to bid him the time of day.

He saw that Billy Jake Foley's flashy black mount was dancing in the grass as the distance closed between them. The sun had finally broken through to glitter brightly on the bridle bits, harness rings and that big .44 in the barrel-chested horseman's large fist. The man appeared cocky and ruthless, Morgan mused, and figured he must be reassured by the fact that his partner was holding Luke helpless and vulnerable under his gun.

Foley suddenly propped and shouted, 'Chip! Are you in there? C'mon out so's we can talk!'

Morgan twisted his head to look as Hannah swung away from him to go rushing across the room to an old closet. Flinging open the door, she grabbed down a battered old Henry rifle and began fumbling for shells. Morgan sprang to his feet and was raising a restraining hand towards the girl when Foley's six-gun thundered and one of the windows caved in with a shimmering, shivering crash.

Diving low, Morgan sighted the sudden white rip that had appeared in the cupboard woodwork barely a couple of feet to Hannah's right. Plainly the hardcase wouldn't see the girl, but his realization of how close that bullet had gone and the way Hannah now stood frozen in terror suddenly enraged him.

These bastards were playing for keeps!

Foley was now riding up and down out front with his smoking six-gun bawling to everyone, 'Git out hy'ar!' when Morgan's Colt barrel snaked through the chink between sill and window. His sights played on past the horseman who was as yet unaware of the danger then focused upon the man holding Luke. Carney was dragging the boy closer and closer to the house now, still with the pistol jammed against his head.

Morgan took aim, slowly counted to three — then squeezed the trigger.

The bullet struck Aaron Carney high up on the right side, just under the armpit. It hit with such savage impact that the man was punched backwards several feet. He righted himself with great effort, lurched drunkenly forwards with his face drained of all colour yet still with the gun clutched tightly in his hand.

For a bad moment a bewildered Luke stood between Morgan's window and Carney. But when the girl screamed at her brother Luke threw himself full-length in the grass just as Carney's finger whitened on the trigger.

Morgan had the hardcase squarely in his sights when his window suddenly exploded, showering him with broken glass.

Billy Jake was buying in.

Two lunging strides carried Morgan to the broken window flanking the front door. Skidding to a halt, he steadied his gunhand against the doorframe and triggered twice, both shots hammering home. Aaron Carney cried out faintly and fell, never feeling the soft kiss of the grass against his cheek.

Now Foley's gun was blasting again, filling Morgan's window with screaming lead, ripping timber and plaster from the frame where he'd been standing.

Instantly Morgan's gun churned. Billy Jake sagged suddenly and clung to his saddle horn in desperation as the animal reared and squealed in terror. But suddenly the man could hold no longer and was howling as he fell.

From the corner of his eye Morgan could still see the girl standing as though turned to stone. Instantly he leapt to the door and flung it wide.

He went through in a low dive — which saved his life. For Foley was on his knees in the grass less than thirty feet distant, both hands holding his six-gun at arm's length and at eye-level, pain-twisted features a study in murderous concentration.

Both men triggered together and a rolling Morgan heard the *thunk* of the other's bullet in the fluted colonnade above his head even as the hardcase's head blew apart beneath that handsome head of jet-black curls.

The merciless gunplay echoed like a beaten gong across the wide grass flats, echoing back faintly from the distant cliffs.

Morgan rose with the gun hanging at his side and a thin plume of smoke rising from the barrel. He didn't bother checking the bodies. He knew where his lead had gone.

He glanced across at Luke, then turned stiffly at the sound of steps to see the girl appear in the doorway. Hannah opened her arms wide and began to run towards him. Although taken by surprise Morgan braced himself for the expected contact which didn't come. Instead the girl rushed right on past, skirts and hair streaming behind to embrace her brother.

The gunfighter's face set in hard lines

as he muttered, ironically, 'Gee, thanks, Mr Morgan . . . Heck, that's all right, Miss . . . all in a day's work . . . think nothing of it.'

★   ★   ★

Morgan sat just inside the barn doorway in a square of sunlight, staring at the Wanted dodgers he'd taken from the dead men's saddle-bags. The beaming, cocky face of Billy Jake Foley and the saturnine features of Aaron Carney stared back at him.

Foley had bounty money tallying just two hundred dollars on his head at various places for cattle rustling. Small time.

Morgan nodded, thinking about Carney. The man had had the look of a genuine tough one, which was the main reason he'd gone after him first, ahead of Foley.

There was a third dodger, and he was studying this with sober interest when he heard the girl call from the house, her voice pure and clear in the cold, sunlit morning.

'Coffee, Mr Morgan!'

He tucked the Wanted dodgers inside his heavy grey shirt and rose from the three-legged stool. Nothing like a bit of gunplay to sharpen a man's taste for strong coffee, he mused with bitter irony.

He glanced across at the stall where a pair of boots protruded from beneath a sheet of stiff canvas. *How many does that tally up to now Morgan?* an inner voice queried. He didn't remember, refused to do so.

He carefully washed the blood from his hands under the pump, then continued on up to the house.

Hannah Garfield had not only fixed coffee but had whipped up a batch of hot biscuits which she served with maple syrup.

Initially, the very sight of food revolted the gunfighter. But after watching Luke bite into his biscuits with gusto for a time he felt a low growling in his belly and found himself reaching for one, then another after that.

The biscuits were excellent, as good as he'd ever tasted. He munched in silence and again reflected upon these strange young people with their golden hair and wide blue eyes. Didn't they fully understand two men had been killed less than an hour ago? Or could it be that they knew, but simply didn't give a damn?

He watched Hannah bite into a second biscuit while her brother looked across the table at him with a smile.

'We really are terribly grateful to you, Mr Morgan,' the girl said.

'Mighty grateful,' affirmed Luke, washing down his food with sweetened coffee. 'Lord only knows what would have happened to us if you hadn't been here.'

Morgan felt himself beginning to relax a little as he reached for another biscuit. At least they were grateful now. Better late than never.

'We can bury them out by the cliffs, Mr Morgan,' Luke said calmly. 'There's plenty of good places out there.'

Morgan lowered his biscuit to the plate untasted, looking from one to the other, surprised again by this seeming indifference to violent death.

Reading his expression, Hannah said, 'Well, we just can't leave them lying about, can we, Mr Morgan?'

'I didn't mean to do that,' he replied. 'I aimed to take them into Mission Fork.'

Brother and sister stopped chewing simultaneously.

'Mission Fork?' the girl said after a silence. 'Oh, you can't do that, Mr Morgan.'

'Why not?' he countered. 'If you shoot somebody you're duty bound to report it to the authorities. You can't just go about putting dead men under the ground and not telling anyone about it. You must be old enough to know that?'

'We know, Mr Morgan,' Luke said

earnestly, leaning forward. 'But you must understand that we simply can't take these men into Mission Fork. Otherwise they will all come rushing out here, swarm all over our ranch.'

'They?' he queried. 'Who are they?'

'People,' replied the boy, and the girl nodded in solemn agreement.

'Citizens,' she said, making the word sound like something distasteful. 'They mustn't come here, Mr Morgan. They must never come here.'

'Damn it, I killed two men with a gun,' Morgan exclaimed, getting to his feet. 'This isn't some fool game being played up here. This is real. There are genuine corpses out there in the barn and it could well be real rope they'll put around all our necks if we don't own up to what happened here today.'

'You don't understand,' Luke countered calmly. 'Nobody ever comes up here, scarce anyone knows that Atlanta even exists. And you can take it from me that nobody will ever be worried about Foley or Carney.'

'Why not?' Morgan said sharply. 'Because they were outlaws?'

Brother and sister exchanged a quick glance. Finally Luke spoke. 'You're just guessing that is what they were.'

'Not really. But while we're on this, where the hell does Chip Greenberry fit into this picture?'

Hannah lowered her gaze to her coffee cup while her brother stared at a bar of sunlight streaming through the window. Neither spoke. Both jumped as the gunfighter slammed his fist down on the table.

'Don't give me that know-nothing look!' he said sharply. 'Carney and Foley were pards of Greenberry and they came up here looking for him. Foley was hollering for him just before the shooting started up. Now you're going to tell me why they figured Greenberry might be up here and why they were prepared to go to such lengths to flush him out!'

'I never heard of anybody named Greenberry,' Luke declared.

Plucking the Wanted dodgers from his shirt, Morgan selected one and unfolded it, placing it down upon a low table. The truebill carried the likeness of a handsome, lean-faced man with slicked-back hair and the thin, pencil-line moustache of a gambler. The information supplied was to the effect that Chip Greenberry was wanted for bank robbery in Colorado, and was known to be riding with Aaron Carney and Billy Jake Foley.

Brother and sister studied the truebill with blank stares, then shook their heads together. 'We don't know this man Greenberry or the others,' Hannah stated calmly.

Morgan slammed his fist on the table, jolting the crockery.

'You're lying!' he accused, jabbing a finger at the girl. 'You wanted me to open up on those two and shoot them down on sight!'

Suddenly he felt totally spent and, lowering himself back into his chair, reached for the coffee pot. Hannah

Garfield leaned across the table and placed a slender hand upon his.

'Mr Morgan, try to understand how it is with Lukey and me up here. People think we're strange, and I suppose we must appear that way. But we really aren't, don't you see? All we ask is that we be left alone, and if we seem callous to you, it's only because life has made us that way. We don't want to hurt anybody and would only ever do so to protect ourselves. Isn't that right, Luke?'

'Solemn truth,' the young man insisted. 'You see, if you take those men back to Mission Fork, it will be all over for us. The sheriff would bring a posse up here to investigate and start asking questions. Next thing you know, everybody would be getting suspicious the way folks always do about others they don't understand. They would find some reason to take us away from here and I'm sure they'd find an excuse to lock us away.'

The girl's eyes suddenly filled with

tears. 'They would part us and cage us simply because we're different, Mr Morgan. We couldn't survive that. We'd rather die.'

The hard lines in Blaze Morgan's face had slowly eased as the girl spoke. And when the first tear fell he believed every word they said and wasn't angry at them any more.

4

High Country

For several minutes no one had spoken in that big, high-ceilinged room. Morgan was on his feet and pacing slowly to and fro, the young couple's eyes never leaving him.

Finally Luke spoke. 'Please, Mr Morgan. They're only a couple of no-good outlaws after all. Nobody will ever miss them.'

Morgan stroked his jaw, knowing he was weakening. Then the girl, after a long silence, said something that startled him.

'You know, despite what you've been saying, I don't think you are all that anxious to deal with the law either, Mr Morgan.'

Luke looked up at his sister sharply. 'What do you mean, Hannah?'

'Yeah, I'd like to know too,' Morgan said warily.

Hannah gestured at the big revolver riding Morgan's right hip. 'I saw how you moved, how you drew that weapon with such speed the moment those men rode up, Mr Morgan. You were ready to fight and even die fighting and it seems to me that a man like that could only be afraid of the law.'

Blaze Morgan smiled a slow, world-weary smile. 'Missy,' he murmured, 'there are worse things than the law to put fear into a man, let me tell you that.'

'Then it's not the law you are running from?' She sounded almost diappointed.

'Nope. But who says I'm running?'

She nodded soberly. 'You're running Mr Morgan. You're running from somebody.'

Annoyance stirred in Morgan. He had always seen running from anything as cowardice, and it riled him to realize that he should seem so transparent to this young girl. But of course he wasn't scared when he'd lit out from Yellow Gulch, Oklahoma, he reassured himself — just unwilling to die for some punk wetback. But he couldn't expect people like this to understand such things, even though it was growing increasingly obvious they were far more perceptive than he'd thought at first.

He rose and moved to the window, fingered the deep gouges in the woodwork where Foley's bullets had come hunting for him.

He shifted his gaze beyond to the still and silent walls of the secret valley. It was possible he'd shaken off Vallinova's killer pack for keeps when chance had led him along that fork in the trail down there in Weeping Woman Valley. It was also possible that quite by accident he had given the slip to that pack of fast guns who had sworn to kill him. And thought, surely all this was not something to jeopardize now by packing two corpses into Mission Fork and thereby announcing to the world — and Juan

Vallinova — just where Blake Morgan was?

After a time, he drew the two Wanted dodgers from inside his shirt and spoke without turning, 'Better break out a couple of shovels, boy.'

★ ★ ★

The wind shifted as they laboured, now coming more from the north and bringing the scent of rain with it. It blew with increasing strength, peppering their faces with specks of gravel.

They had tamped earth flat over the new graves, then replaced the sods they had cut out of this remote section at the base of the cliffs. Above, a lone buzzard which had followed the entire operation with bright-eyed interest, finally gave up and glided away in search of an easier feast someplace else.

Wind and rain would soon erase whatever traces they might have left behind, and the graves would be lost in the green valley forever.

Luke Garfield and Blaze Morgan stood with heads briefly bowed. The boy had been surprised when the gunfighter had insisted on a prayer. But Morgan had an unchanging rule about the dead. He never saw a man buried without the benefit of prayer, hoping that when his day came, he himself would not be laid away without at least a few words that might somehow shoehorn him into Paradise.

Many a bitter and bloody enemy of Blaze Morgan would have been astonished to know the gunman actually believed in a life hereafter.

'Do you want to say the words, kid?' Morgan asked.

'I don't know any.'

Morgan nodded. That figured.

So, leaning his hands on his shovel, he murmured a few brief words, and the other murmured, 'Amen.'

Morgan replaced his hat and went back to the horses. Mounting up, he sent the youth on ahead of him. He wanted time alone to think. Not about

Foley and Carney now, for they had passed into history. He had to consider his next move, the immediate future of Blake Morgan.

Should he stay on a spell here?

That was the question he turned over in his mind as the boisterous wind buffeted him. Atlanta was remote and little-known according to the Garfields. It was possible that he could just stay put here a week or two, then drift on again without having hellions breathing down his neck.

Of course it was plain that the Garfields wanted him gone just as soon as possible; there was also the risk they might try something as they had done at daybreak should he elect to extend his stay. Or maybe not? Sure, they were a couple of strange ones. But they still owed him and that might hold them from trying something foolish.

He decided to defer a decision until later. He halted the horse, turned his back to the wind and built a cigarette. Trailing smoke over one shoulder, he continued on, tugging up his collar against the sharpening blast of the icy wind.

It would snow soon, he mused — just another reason for him to stay put up here.

★   ★   ★

He skirted a high shelf then steered the horse through a scatter of giant boulders and started up the slope of a low hill.

Soon it was possible to make out the distant bulk of the great house rising abruptly from the valley floor. He'd questioned the boy about many things as they worked on the graves, and the house and its history were among the few topics the boy had been prepared to discuss.

He'd learned that the mansion had been built some twenty years earlier by the boy's maternal grandmother, a high-born southern lady who had spent a small fortune in recreating her own version of a Mississippi mansion in the lonely splendour of the Flintlock Mountains.

Here the woman had lived the life of a recluse, pining for her deceased husband, fretting over the North-South troubles which had been the cause of her leaving Georgia and worrying ceaselessly about her only daughter and two grandchildren.

Luke had not explained why the old woman had worried about them so constantly, had in fact refused to discuss his parents at all.

Morgan could only guess the grandmother had died and left the Atlanta ranch to her daughter and family. But as to what had befallen the parents, or how long Luke and Hannah had been living alone up here, he had no notion.

No more than he understood the reason why that pair of gun thugs should have seemed so certain they would find their partner, the elusive Chip Greenberry, at Atlanta.

Light snow was blurring the outline of the great house as Morgan led the way in past the corrals and headed for the barn.

He was peeved when he glimpsed the mule and horses still in the corral, standing in a miserable, huddled bunch with their tails to the weather. He was tempted to go to the house and drag Luke out to take care of stabling the animals, but let it go. He would likely handle the chore quicker alone anyway.

He'd not figured on dealing with a critter as cantankerous as the ancient mule, Jupiter. As soon as he entered the corral the bottle-nose started in snorting and pawing the earth like some wild equine king of the high country. Morgan was in no mood for any of this as he roped the critter then hauled it off for the stables.

He was sweating slightly by the time he was through. He quit the stables and the rising wind buffeted him as he trudged towards the house. He realized he was looking around for the dog, but it was no place to be seen. Then, as he was passing the gloomy bulk of the smithy, he heard a low whimpering.

With a frown, he changed direction and ducked beneath the low doorway of the smithy. The place was gloomy and filled with the smell of cold ashes and rusted metal. He saw the anvil, bedded into a thick tree stump next to a cooling tub half-filled with oily water. Tongs, hammers, files and scraps of iron cluttered the nearby bench, and beyond the anvil was a low brick hearth cradling a bed of dead ashes.

The dog lay by the ashes, its whimpering silenced now as it saw Morgan standing there.

Man and animal exchanged a long look before Morgan noticed the ashes had been disturbed. The dog had been digging there.

But why?

With a frown he bent and reached into the forge. When he fingered the ashes, the dog leapt up eagerly and started digging furiously.

Morgan watched curiously. He realized the dog had not come near the house or its two young occupants since his arrival. It obviously belonged to somebody, and it was just as plain that the animal was fretting.

For whom?

His eyes now fully accustomed to the gloom, Morgan slowly became aware of other things. He realized the hearth area appeared sunken and the earth surrounding it appeared softer than elsewhere. He estimated the slightly depressed sector to be some ten feet long by three wide.

He stood motionless for a time with dark suspicions stirring in his mind like coiled snakes. Abruptly, he drove his boot heels into the earth by the bricks and his frown cut deeper when he saw how easily it gave way. The dog had quit whimpering and stared up at him expectantly.

A shovel leaned against the wall close by. He hesitated a moment before snatching it up. He spat on his palms and started digging.

He kept working until a flash of

colour appeared between his feet. Kneeling, he carefully scraped away some further loosened earth until seeing that what he was uncovering was a check shirt.

A little more scraping — and the body of a man lay exposed. The corpse was that of a tall and powerfully built man of around forty with a face deeply seamed by hard living, so it appeared. He'd not been dead long. Apart from the gaping bullet wound in the chest, there were no other injuries. He'd been buried fully clothed and had been backshot.

The dog whimpered and Morgan reached out to rub its neck.

'Friend of yours, partner?' he murmured, then reached down and drew the six-gun from the dead man's holster.

The weapon was a single-action Colt. It had a faded yellow ivory grip that was worn smooth. The sheen was long gone from the metal leaving it grey and dull in the feeble light of the smithy.

Morgan turned the gun upside down and saw there was a name engraved on the base-plate.

The name was Jesse Garfield.

*   *   *

In the gloomy upper reaches of the house Hannah Garfield closed and carefully locked the door of the small attic room behind her, then slipped the key into the slash pocket of her dress before going downstairs.

On the first-floor landing the girl paused to stare from the tall, crescent-shaped windows at the swirling snow outside. The wind was murmuring in the chimney with a sound like soft voices and she heard the branches of the cottonwood at the southern end of the house brushing restlessly against the walls.

Craning her neck now, she stared off in the direction of the outbuildings to see if she might catch a glimpse of Blaze Morgan, but the big man was no

77

place to be seen.

Somewhere below a door opened and closed and she heard her brother's footsteps as he came along the corridor towards the room which their grand-mother had designed as an elegant parlour, but which they had turned into an all-purpose living-room.

Lifting up her skirts, Hannah went quickly downstairs and crossed the lobby to the big room. As she entered, Luke was taking cold flapjacks from a platter and placing them in a battered cannister.

'Didn't he eat anything?' Hannah asked.

'Nothing.'

The girl twisted her hands. 'What are we going to do about him, Lukey?' Her voice was normal now, a young woman's cultivated tones. It was only in the presence of outsiders that brother and sister adopted that strange, flat monotone.

Luke appeared older than his seven-teen years as he sat down at a big, rough table, a boy burdened by cares and responsibilities that seemed to be growing heavier by the day, the hour.

'Right now, it's not so much him we have to worry about, Sis, as Morgan.'

Hannah forced a smile as she moved to the stove to put on coffee. She could tell her brother was dejected and she saw it as her duty to cheer him up as she had always done since their mother died.

'I'm quite sure Mr. Morgan will soon move on and leave us in peace, Lukey,' she said confidently, filling the pot from a cracked water pitcher. 'He is a gunfighter and they aren't the kind to stay in any one place too long.'

'But what if he doesn't move on?'

'Then we shall just have to be patient and wait, won't we?' Luke was clenching his hands upon the oilcloth. 'The man scares me, Sis. The way he handles guns and all . . . He's too much like . . . well, you know.'

'Hush, Lukey!' she admonished, coming to the table to rest a hand on his shoulder. 'I'm quite sure he means us no harm.'

'I don't trust him. I don't trust anybody but you, Hannah. If he doesn't quit . . . then we might have to try again . . .'

'You shouldn't say things like that after what he did for us today.'

'Maybe it wasn't for us, Sis. The man is running from something or somebody, and it could be he reckoned Foley and Carney might be after him.'

The girl's expression turned pensive as she brushed a strand of bright golden hair from her brow. She turned to the stove. 'I'd rather we didn't have to . . . whatever it was you were just saying, Lukey. Not if there's any other way.'

'The man is mighty curious about us, you can tell. You should have heard the questions he asked me out at the cliffs. Matter of fact he asked so many I got to wondering if he had got wind of the money.'

The girl turned towards him, but

before she could reply, steps sounded on the front gallery. Heavy steps. Two pairs of eyes swung to the door as the steps halted. Next moment the door burst open and an apparition stood there in the gloomy half-light against a wild backdrop of whirling snow. In the uncertain light it looked like a man with a grotesquely huge and misshapen upper body, but as he moved in, pushed by the wind that gusted snow halfway across the room, they realized it was Blaze Morgan with a body draped across his shoulders.

Still without a word, Morgan heaved his burden forward. The dead man landed with a sickening thud on the threadbare carpet, and the moment she saw the white face framed by mud-streaked yellow hair, Hannah Garfield moaned softly and crumpled against the wall.

'Sis!' Luke's voice was laced with alarm as he started towards the girl's slumped figure. But suddenly Morgan was blocking his path. The gunfighter's face was like something hewn from granite.

'Your sister's just passed out, kid — but you start talking!'

Luke backed up from Morgan's drilling stare, away from the stiffened corpse. His lips worked but no sound came. With his back pressed against a wall, he watched Morgan lift his sister as easily as if she were a child, then place her upon the battered old sofa. Hannah's eyelids fluttered and the gunfighter touched her cheek gently before turning his accusing stare back to the youth.

'You are not talking, kid,' he growled. He jabbed a finger at the body. 'Who is that?'

Hannah sat up sharply, her face still ashen but her eyes sharp and alert again. 'We've never seen this man before, have we, Luke?'

As though strengthened by his sister's poise and strength, Luke inhaled deeply, straightened his shoulders and met Morgan's stormy eyes levelly.

'Never!' he affirmed.

'Liar!' Morgan snapped. 'You're both lying!' He reached under his jacket and produced the silver-barrelled, single-action Colt with the yellowed ivory grip. He tapped the inscription on the butt. 'Jesse Garfield,' he said accusingly. 'Your father, I take it?'

Neither answered. Two pairs of blue eyes were focused upon the weapon, as though mesmerized. Realizing the weapon was having the opposite effect to that which he'd hoped for, Morgan thrust the weapon back out of sight in his belt before moving across to stand by the dead man.

'How did your father die?' he demanded again, in a quieter tone.

'That isn't our father, Mr Morgan,' the girl stated.

'The gun, the colour of his hair, and the fact that you two youngsters are living here all alone and scared of your own shadows tells me he surely is, missy!' he countered.

Hannah paused by the boarded-up

window and stared beseechingly at her brother. The whole house shook to a violent gust and beyond the windows now the whole world was an opaque and seething world of white. Dragging his gaze away from the girl, Luke met Morgan's intimidating stare for a long moment, finally sighed and shook his head.

'It's no use, Sis,' he said. 'He knows . . . '

'Then, this is your father?' Morgan pressed.

'Was,' Luke corrected.

'How did he die?'

'We don't know.'

'You're lying again!'

That was the truth. Luke Garfield was lying. And he went right on lying and shaking his head in response to every question an increasingly exasperated Morgan fired at him during the next harrowing minutes until the gunfighter finally cursed and threw his hands up in resignation.

'All right — all goddamn right!' he

said angrily, and, bending from the waist, he hefted the dead man and threw him across one shoulder with effortless ease, started for the door. 'You don't leave me any choice.'

'What do you mean to do?' Luke called uneasily.

Morgan glanced back once before reefing the door open. They barely heard his reply before the heavy door banged shut behind him: 'Go see the law, what else?'

It was intensely quiet in the room after he had gone, almost as though he had taken the sullen sounds of the storm with him and the dead man. A stick of wood crackled in the stove and Hannah jumped, startled by the sound, then smiled at her own nervousness. The smile faded when she saw the desperate expression on her brother's face.

'I-I think you were right, Lukey,' she said reassuringly. 'Concerning what we must do, that is. Morgan won't be able to leave for Mission Fork before first light in the morning at the earliest. That gives us plenty of time to stop him.'

'No . . . '

Luke Garfield ran his fingers through his hair with a weary gesture. Half an hour earlier it had been he who had suggested they might be forced to kill the big intruder to Atlanta, his sister who had argued against it. Now positions were reversed. Earlier, Luke had honestly believed he could go through with his proposal, if he must. But the grisly spectacle of his father's disinterred body and the realization that their terrible secret was out, had left him feeling drained and very young. And that was surely no way to feel for any man contemplating rubbing out big Blaze Morgan. 'We couldn't handle it, Sis,' he said huskily. 'We'd both just likely wind up dead.'

Hannah lifted her chin. 'Then they'll hang us, Lukey.'

He twitched. 'Maybe they won't.'

'Yes, they will. They'll hang us both unless we stop Morgan getting to town.'

The young man stared at his sister and felt himself drawing from her deeper well of strength again. 'I'll think on it, Sis,' he said, then went to the closet and took out the rifle there, the oil and the cloth. He always thought better when he had something to occupy his hands. Seating himself at the big mahogany table, he went to work silently and efficiently cleaning the weapon. The girl sat still as stone, seemingly unable to take her gaze from the battered old rifle which had ended her father's life.

5

All Night Long

In the darkness of the quiet, picture-book night with thick white snowflakes falling about him, Blaze Morgan crossed the ranch yard leaving deep footprints in the snow. The wind had dropped completely and showed no sign of picking up again. Beneath a low sky, now covered in snow clouds which reflected the glow from the mansion lights, the big man moved slowly, feeling the touch of snowflakes against his sun-browned face.

There was something peaceful about a snowy night like this, even here — the sort of night that made it easy to think of Grace . . .

★　★　★

Denver, Colorado — midwinter 1867. That was where it had begun and, to all intents and purposes, ended. It was love at first sight at the Governor's Ball, both for the prettiest schoolmarm in all of Denver and the man of mystery named Blaze Morgan, and love had flourished during those three bright months of a high-plains winter. But springtime brought more than a budding and flowering of the high country that year; it brought a hawk-featured man named Dancey with a tied-down gun and one thousand dollars to be earned if he could kill a man named Morgan.

Until that sunny morning when he'd faced hired gun Joe Dancey down and blasted him into eternity, Morgan had actually come to believe he had quit the dangerous trade of the fast gun. He held down a job as a blacksmith, there was money in the bank, the governor called him by his given name. But Dancey's blood washed all that away for in the wake of the fatal gunfight came publicity from far distant places, and both Denver and Grace Perrell became aware that Blaze Morgan was now regarded as a gunfighter, a man who killed for money.

This was never how Morgan had wanted it, but soon realized it was out of his hands. The man he'd gunned down was famous for his gunskills, now Morgan was equally famous, and gunslingers sought him out for money, for excitement, for the kind of glory that went with the title, 'fast gun'.

There was no escape. For now he had the name and wherever he went men whispered behind their hands and the newspapers gave unstinting space to every gun battle he was forced to fight — or else be branded yellow. He tried hiding and changing his name. He even tried refusing to meet a challenge. But sooner or later 'he' would appear — the stranger with the hawk features and low-slung gun. And he would find himself facing the grim option again: fight or die.

And up in Denver Grace read about each man he shot down and could never understand that he had to go on killing while men still challenged him.

As time went by, Grace only thought about Blaze when she read or heard he'd fought again . . . and won . . .

Morgan returned to the present with a jolt, seeing that his daydreaming had caused him to walk right on by the stables. Halting, he shook his head sharply and Grace's lovely image was gone. He took a deep breath and, bending down, scooped up a large handful of snow. He rubbed his face with it, tasted it and felt he had somehow been cleansed.

Returning to the stables he went inside and lit a lantern. The interior sprang from the darkness as he turned up the wick and his gaze cut directly to the stall where Jesse Garfield lay under the same sheet of stiff canvas he'd used earlier for Carney and Foley.

His mount whickered a greeting. He took down the curry comb and walked to the stall, swaying to avoid snapping mule teeth when the ill-tempered Jupiter took a bite at him as he passed by.

The appaloosa didn't really need grooming, as Morgan had taken care of that chore earlier. But he sensed time was going to hang heavy on his hands tonight. Sleep was out of the question. Having told Luke and Hannah of his plans, he had no intention of falling asleep and giving them another chance to do what they'd failed to accomplish that morning.

The chore completed he next went to work on the ranch horses, eventually pausing to check his watch. Ten o'clock. Still early. There had been no sign of the Garfields when he left the house after supper, but he did not believe they would have retired. He sensed they were around someplace, most likely keeping a close watch on the stables was his guess. He could picture them whispering and plotting in the night, trying to decide whether they could kill him the way it seemed they might have slain their father . . .

Morgan sighed as he shrugged into his sheepskin jacket. He hoped they didn't try anything. Somehow he'd avoided gunning anyone under twenty-one years of age during his career and didn't want to break that record either here in the Flintlocks or anyplace else.

Going out again he perched on a crate against the darkened stable door and built himself a cigarette. With the smoke going to his satisfaction he tilted his head back against the wall and watched the great house.

It was tough things had turned out the way they had, he mused. For he still clung to the belief that this place might well have made the best hideaway a man like him could ever hope to find. Not just someplace to wait out Vallinova, but somewhere where a man could maybe settle down and hang up the guns for good, leaving folks elsewhere to speculate on whatever fate might have befallen Blaze Morgan.

He smiled faintly. Some chance of

that ever happening! The Atlanta might be remote from the world but all the dangers and defects of mankind were still to be found here. In twenty-four hours he had been forced to kill two men, dug up another's corpse and had probably uncovered a case of patricide. Even the fast guns and wild hell-raisers of Dodge City would have been content with a high run of trouble like that.

A dark shape appeared against the snow near the smithy. Morgan snapped his fingers and Jesse Garfield's dog came across to him, squatted at his side. Morgan stroked the animal's neck. 'Too bad you can't talk, old-timer, on account I sure would have a mess of questions to put to you before I take your master's corpse to town.'

The dog licked his hand and managed a sad wag of the tail. They sat together in the darkness and watched the snowflakes fall silently over house, hill and barn.

It was a fair spell later when Morgan heard a faint sound from the direction of the house. He stirred and fingered gun butt. He could see the front doors clearly — no sign of life there. He switched his gaze to the rear as he rose, and the dog pricked its ears and emitted a low growl.

He silenced the animal with a touch and it went several steps forward then halted. Its ears were pricked and it appeared to be staring fixedly at the blank side wall of the building. Morgan saw nothing, at first. Then the sound was repeated and he identified it as stone against stone.

The mansion's foundations were cut from granite.

The Colt was in his fist as he started across the open space of the yard. He moved slowly, sharp eyes cutting left and right. He was passing by the corrals with their snow-crested posts and rails when he propped in his tracks. A slab of stone had just tumbled down from the three-feet high foundation wall and rolled in the snow, leaving a dark square behind which was immediately filled by the head and shoulders of a man.

Morgan froze as the figure wriggled through the aperture, dropped, then got to his feet in the snow. By then, Morgan knew who it was he was staring at.

Chip Greenberry!

Morgan went forward and the figure froze in his tracks.

'Who the hell . . . ?' he began, then turned to run.

'Hold — or eat lead, scum!'

The command saw Greenberry falter, then brought him to a stop. Turning to face Morgan the man's hands were spread out from his sides, gunfighter style. Yet Greenberry wore no weapons.

Halting several feet away, Morgan glanced at the hole in the foundation wall and realized there must be a cellar beneath the mansion. But if that was the case, what in hell was Greenberry doing in it?

At that moment Greenberry found his voice. He sounded angry and bitter as he said, 'Who the hell are you, lawman?'

Morgan didn't respond immediately, raking the man up and down with his eyes. Greenberry was tall and lean with good shoulders. He was dressed expensively but his garb showed signs of rough wear. He noted that his hands were chafed and bleeding, just as you might expect if somebody had been hard at work dislodging a block of stone.

'Name's Morgan,' he said at length, moving closer. 'No, I'm not law, Greenberry. But I know who and what you are.' He indicated the hole in the wall. 'What the hell were you doing down there?'

Greenberry's narrow face darkened.

'Those loco brats shut me down there after they gunned their daddy down — ' He broke off, shaking, sleeved his mouth before he went on. 'I've been locked up down there for days, expecting every hour to be my last while I was rasping away at the mortar holding that block in place . . . ' He slumped back against the wall. 'I been through hell, pure hell.'

Morgan drew closer.

'You say Luke and Hannah Garfield killed their father?'

'Damn right. Buckshot him down right out there in front of the house in broad daylight.' He waved his hands. 'Do you have to point that thing at me, Morgan?'

Morgan lowered the Colt. 'Tell me everything, mister. What led up to the shooting, what you were doing here, everything.'

Greenberry's eyes narrowed. He was a dangerous man yet didn't look it as he began to speak. He acted more like a simple man, glad to be alive and maybe to have found a friend.

'Me and Jesse tied one on in Mission Fork last Saturday night, and he invited me to do a little elk hunting in the high country. When we got here there was a big argument between Jesse and his limp-brained kids about him wasting money on liquor and such like. Well, I was thinking of moseying when the boy comes up with a shooter and lets Jesse have one right in the back.' He grimaced. 'Glory be. You should have seen the hole that old rifle bullet made coming out.'

'I did,' Morgan muttered. 'I found Garfield's body today. It's in the stables now. I'm taking it down to Mission Fork come morning. Reckon I'll take you with me. They'll want a witness.'

It was at that moment that Luke Garfield suddenly appeared around the corner of the house clutching a rifle. The youth started at seeing Greenberry. As Morgan turned to confront the boy Greenberry drove his shoulder into him and snatched the Colt from his fingers.

Staggering, almost falling, Morgan saw the six-gun sweeping up — saw the outlaw's fierce grimace as he began to squeeze trigger. Morgan plunged his hand down his pants top and his fingers closed around the butt of the derringer, even though he figured he had little hope of getting it clear before Greenberry triggered.

In the next instant, the boom of a shot shattered the snowy night.

But Morgan wasn't hit. It was Garfield who'd triggered, and he'd fired at Greenberry. The shot was aimed at the outlaw's heart but it missed its mark to rip through the sweep of muscle beneath his arm.

It was not a stopping shot but was enough to send Greenberry reeling, fighting to regain his balance. Morgan's hand jerked clear of his pants top and the derringer spat crimson bore flame as Greenberry again got set to shoot. Morgan aimed for the heart and rarely missed his target. But by this time the outlaw had moved out of the tiny weapon's restricted range and the bullet's lethal force was spent by the time it punched into Greenberry's ribs.

Even so, it was a telling blow which caused the hardcase to go down on one knee. Morgan started towards him but Greenberry kicked to his hands and knees, came erect and rushed from sight beyond the corner of the house.

Morgan backed up.

A derringer was no match for a Colt .45.

Flattening against the house wall, derringer cocked and ready, he beckoned urgently to the youth who promptly came floundering through the snow towards him.

'He's hit, Mr Morgan. We both hit him!'

'He's still dangerous,' Morgan stated, seizing the rifle. 'Now get back inside and you and your sister keep out of sight while I deal with him.'

'You might need help, Mr Morgan. He's a mighty mean man.'

'Get!' Morgan rapped, and didn't wait to argue any longer as he lunged for the rear of the mansion. As he approached the corner where Greenberry had disappeared he dropped belly flat, then peered around with his head barely inches above ground level, the rifle extended beneath him.

No fiery gunblast greeted him. Distant movement caught his eye and he made out a dark shape moving up the snowy slope of the first hill beyond the house a hundred yards distant.

Surging erect, Morgan levelled the rifle at an angle well above the outlaw's head and triggered twice, but the man didn't even turn.

'We'll have to go after him, Mr Morgan,' a voice panted at his elbow. 'There's nothing out there for Greenberry but cold and snow. He'll head back here as soon as he gets the chance and we mightn't be so lucky next time.'

Morgan considered this and finally nodded. Greenberry wasn't dressed for cold conditions and the man was losing blood. He would come back with that Colt, likely just as soon as the wind rose to give him enough cover.

Morgan was grim jawed and resolute as he started for the hill at a lunging walk, but slowed at the sound of footsteps behind. He turned sharply. 'Go look to your sister, boy,' he said gruffly.

Luke halted, pale and concerned. 'But, Mr Morgan, you might need me. Greenberry's a killer.'

'So am I, son,' Morgan retorted with surprising bitterness as he turned away. 'So am I . . .'

* * *

It was very quiet in the hills, no sound at all as the snow drifted down.

The footprints stretching away before Morgan were deeply etched in the snow. Too deep, the gunfighter mused suspiciously. Dropping to one knee he examined the prints closely, then grunted. Smart! His man had indeed crossed this snowy slope but had then backed up over his own footprints!

Every sense clamouring, he threw himself headlong downslope a split-second before the Colt roared from the brushline. He felt lead scorch his ribs. He made no attempt to return fire but instead kept rolling over and over downslope towards a deep gulch. The hidden gunman punched two further shots at him before the ground fell away beneath him and he was plunging into the narrow, icy stream.

He was in the water then out of it all in one breath-snapping second. Ignoring the cold, he came up in a low crouch, snaked along the bed of the gulch before daring to raise his head.

No sign of life along the brushline.

He waited a full half-minute to be certain all was clear, then clambered his way back up the flank.

Reaching the top, Morgan grunted as a gust of freezing air struck his face. The wind was rising. Casting about for a sign in the gloom, at last he picked up the single set of footprints angling east and began following them down the lee of the hill.

He checked out a possible ambush site, then another. By now the wind was steady and the snow was beginning to swirl again. His heart was thudding against his rib cage as he moved on. The urge to hurry was strong but he refused to do so. Just as well. He figured he'd covered another twenty cautious yards when, far upslope, a frozen branch snapped loud as a gunshot.

Darting across open space, Morgan reached a nest of boulders. He dived in, came up on both elbows, squinted intently as further sounds came from upslope. Greenberry was making a hell of a racket up there. How come?

Morgan scanned his surrounds until he spotted a a deep gully angling upwards. His guess was that Greenberry was likely somewhere along that fissure, making a racket in the hope of luring him up there into an ambush. Briefly, Morgan was tempted to scout around the gully and attempt to come in on his man from the flank but then decided against it.

He moved behind the cover of a sturdy birch, hugging it close so his silhouette would not be seen. Snow slid silently from the leaves overhead. It was cold as charity and his wet garb was freezing up. He was next to certain Greenberry knew where he was, just as he believed the outlaw could have nailed him earlier had he been armed with a rifle instead of a six-gun. There was no doubting the man wanted him dead and done with, but what that reason could be he had no idea.

The wind moaned softly in the trees. Time dragged by and Morgan was considering quitting before he froze solid, when he heard the faint click of metal upon stone.

Calmly he raised the rifle barrel to waist height, ready to jerk it to his shoulder in an instant.

A long moment of silence was broken by another furtive sound, and Morgan yelled, 'Reach, outlaw!'

Dimly he made out the shape of the man a moment before the leaping stab of fire whipped overhead and he heard the smashing thud of the slug striking stone directly behind, showering him with bark splinters.

He fired back, and the outlaw made

his mistake. He dived sideways for better cover and in that split-second Morgan triggered . . . and the body of the outlaw came tumbling downslope through the snow, the smoking gun beneath him.

Morgan crouched low and waited. In the bad light he could not be certain where his bullet had gone. He made no sound, listening to the wind; there was nothing else to be heard.

Suddenly the dark shape came alive.

The shot was a dart of leaping flame and a brutal concussion of sound. A lethal finger tugged at his jacket collar as he returned fire, slamming a single shot into the outlaw's body.

This time there was no risk in quitting cover. Morgan found Greenberry dead with his last bullet in his heart.

6

Raging Guns

Jesse Garfield, Aaron Carney, Billy Jake Foley — and now Chip Greenberry.

No doubt about it. For a place in the high country which Blake Morgan had once envisioned as a peaceful, remote retreat for a world-weary man of the gun, Atlanta Ranch was proving the bloodied opposite.

There were places down along the borderlands Morgan knew of where even children toted guns, and drunken judges issued death sentences for trivial offences on a whim. None of these could have been any more lethal than Atlanta Ranch right now.

Such were his thoughts as the tall man mounted the creaking stairs of the big house. In the wake of the shoot-out in the hills he'd returned to the headquarters, changed out of his frozen gear, then headed back out on a fresh horse to retrieve Greenberry's body, now lying in the stables with Jesse Garfield's remains. It was no longer snowing and the world beyond the house was a shimmering, unsullied white.

In his quarters Morgan peeled off his sheepskin and tossed his hat onto the bed. He unbuckled the gunbelt and hung it on the back of the chair, then took out the silver-mounted derringer won in a poker game with Kit Carson in Tucson a year earlier.

Morgan hefted the ugly little weapon thoughtfully. He'd reached a stage where he'd lost count of the actual number of times this sneak shooter had saved his life, and now could add Chip Greenberry to that growing list.

With a grunt he replaced the derringer in its soft leather holster snugged in behind his large, horse-shaped belt buckle. He propped the chair against the door handle then sat down to go over the dead man's relics.

Greenberry had gone to his reward in posession of two Red Man cigars in an engraved silver tin, thirty-seven cents in cash, a woman's garter with a red rosette and the worn-down stub of the food fork he'd used to scrape his way to freedom from his basement prison. He'd also left behind the unanswered question — had he told the truth about the Garfields?

Setting the pathetic collection aside, Morgan massaged his brow thoughtfully before rising. He flexed his powerful body while crossing to the window. He knew from the Wanted dodgers on Billy Jake Foley that Greenberry was a hunted outlaw, and certainly had shown himself to be both treacherous and murderous last night.

Not the breed on whom a man would want to place too much reliance, obviously. Yet surely the same assessment could be applied to his strange young hosts.

The light was strengthening every moment now. Roosters crowed and flapped their wings out back and deep in the stables the ancient Jupiter was to be heard kicking the sawdust out of his stall. Everything seemed everyday and normal — which was about as wrong as appearances could be.

This was the day he would put an end to all mysteries — so Blaze Morgan pledged himself.

Reflecting, he could now see there had been times when he'd thought the Garfields might be merely scared and desperate victims of unknown circumstances.

But in the light of last night it seemed sympathy was a luxury he could no longer afford.

Today he planned on riding down to Mission Fork despite the snowdrifts. He would reveal what he knew then leave it to the law to sort out the dark and bloody mysteries of this place.

He suddenly sniffed and snapped alert. Someone was frying bacon. Yet there'd been no sign of the Garfields upon his return to the house and he'd not bothered searching for them. The mansion had felt empty but this scent told him there had to be *someone* around.

He buckled on the gun again, jaw muscles working. He paused momentarily to scowl at the dead man's pathetic possessions. Then he scooped up his hat, shifted the chair he'd employed as a brace aside and stepped out with six-gun in hand.

He glanced left and right along the hallway before going to the stairs and starting down. He didn't believe the Garfields would be loco enough to make an attempt on his life, but still wouldn't be taking any chances.

He found Hannah standing at the battered old stove which was glowing cherry-red through the vent holes and filled the room with its warmth. The girl wore a patched blue dress with a flowered apron tied around her slender waist as she turned bacon and eggs in a heavy skillet.

She acknowledged his presence with the faintest of nods. 'Take your place,

Mr Morgan. I'll have your breakfast ready in a moment.'

Her voice was flat, her expression as blank as the day they'd met.

'Where's your brother?' he demanded, moving to the side window to jerk back the drapes.

'Feeding the stock.'

He turned to study her, the scar on his neck noticeably white against his bronzed skin.

'I killed a man,' he stated flatly. 'Another one.'

'Lukey told me.'

She turned from the stove with a tin platter overflowing with hot food. She set it on the table and placed cutlery within reach before returning to the stove.

The mood he was in, Morgan was tempted to tell her to go straight to hell with her breakfast. But he was way too hungry for that. And taking up a knife and fork, he thought sardonically there was nothing like killing to put an edge on a man's appetite.

He was halfway through eating when Luke showed up. The youth shrugged out of a heavy woollen jacket, nodded absently to him, then crossed to the stove to warm his hands.

Morgan studied the boy's back for a long moment, then speared a rasher of bacon and forked it into his mouth. There was no doubt in Morgan's mind that but for his intervention Chip Greenberry would have paid his captors in gunsmoke last night. The Garfields knew this also, but gratitude was plainly not their long suit.

Brother and sister stood close together talking in low voices for some minutes, but when they came to the table to eat they fell silent.

Gazing from one to the other, Morgan nodded. OK. If this was how they wanted to play their childish games, he would go along with it. Eventually they would talk to the law, and he would be there to hear what was said then.

Yet he'd no sooner decided on this

than Luke Garfield spoke up. 'What will you do now, Mr Morgan?'

He made no response. Shoving his plate from him, he leaned back in his chair and took out his tobacco. He rolled his cigarette one-handed, the right resting upon the butt of the Navy Colt below table level. The siblings watched him light his cigarette and draw deeply. He hooked a thumb in his broad belt and stared back at them in frosty silence.

Luke and Hannah traded glances. Then the boy said, 'Did Greenberry tell you anything, Mr Morgan?'

Morgan was bored with his game already, but now his curiosity was piqued.

Rising, he crossed to the pot-belly and stood with his back to the heat. 'He told me you two murdered your father.'

They seemed shocked. The girl said, 'And you believe that?'

'It doesn't matter what I believe. I'll leave it to the Mission Fork law to sort that out.'

'It will mean the end for Hannah and me if you go to the law, Mr Morgan,' Luke said in an unemotional voice.

'You should have thought of that before you started back-shooting folks and locking men in cellars.'

Their food untouched before them, brother and sister stared at the gunfighter for a long minute in silence. With his heavy shoulders straining against the seams of the threadbare shirt he'd found in the stables, the Colt sagging from its holster and his broad brown face set stone hard, Morgan made as formidable a sight as either had ever seen.

A lengthy silence. Suddenly Luke nodded to his sister, got up and crossed to the battered old sofa. He stooped and felt beneath the cushions.

He froze abruptly at the sound of a Colt hammer clicking back.

'Just what are you doing there, kid?' Morgan wanted to know.

'Just getting the money.'

Morgan's eyes widened. 'Money? What money?'

Luke came erect clutching a small canvas sack. 'There's one thousand dollars here, Mr Morgan. Will you take that in return for not going to the law about us?'

A scowling Morgan said nothing until the youth crossed the room and opened the drawstring of the sack to dump the contents upon the table. Ten fat bundles of banknotes lay under the light.

Morgan put his piece away and went to the table. He picked up a bundle of bills and fingered through it. One hundred dollars. Each bundle was of an identical size. He was indeed looking at a thousand dollars in cash.

He didn't have to ask how they had come by it. His expression demanded it. Yet he failed to get what he wanted. The siblings were quite prepared to pay him the money for his silence — more if he wanted it, so Luke said. But they would not divulge its source.

Morgan decided to test them out. 'Maybe I could be bought,' he told them. 'But it would take much more to quieten my conscience.'

The pair conferred and then Hannah quit the room to return several minutes later with a much larger sack than the first. This bag contained nine thousand in cash. She said Morgan could have it all providing he would agree to saddle up and ride out, forgetting he'd ever set foot in a place called Atlanta Ranch.

Most might have been tempted, but not Blaze Morgan. All this achieved for him was a hardening of the conviction that the law, and only the law, could ever unravel the mystery surrounding the Garfields, their late father, and three dead outlaws.

Luke appeared to accept his decision well enough when he announced he was heading for Mission Fork immediately. Yet as he turned for the door he saw Hannah's pretty face crumple, the bright sheen of tears in her eyes.

The girl began to cry as he stepped out on to the gallery. He closed the heavy, bullet-scarred door behind him, then stood with his head angled low, listening to the young woman weeping.

* * *

Riding down over the snow-covered slopes, Blaze Morgan couldn't help but be aware of the beauty of that high valley. With a sigh, he reached for his tobacco sack, but didn't get to use it. Instead he reined the appaloosa up sharply to stare down at fresh hoof-prints in the snow.

To draw his gun before inspecting the sign was an instinctive reaction. He sat in his saddle and looked about him on every side. He saw snow, dark trees and tawny cliffs. There was also another set of clear hoofprints coming from the pass at the north end of the valley and angling away south-east.

He sat motionless for a long time. He was tempted to ride on and just forget what he had seen, but knew he could not. Not with so many unanswered questions and mysteries hanging in the air, he couldn't. There was also the concern that tracks could well mean danger of some kind to the young ranchers, who, though strange, seemed to him entirely vulnerable.

It was curious — so he reflected later — that Vallinova didn't even enter his mind until some twenty minutes later when, having followed the sign for several miles, he glimpsed two men up ahead brewing coffee over a small sullen fire.

He'd not seen either before yet guessed they could easily be owlhoot, judging by their weaponry and flashy Mexican garb.

Sprawled belly-flat behind a snow-crusted patch of sage on the rim of a low rise, the horse tethered in a draw behind him, Morgan studied the pair intently and absorbed every detail.

The first man was small and quick, dark-complexioned, with restless eyes and slender limbs. When he spoke Morgan realized he was American. Seated across the fire from him his companion was a powerful hulk with a moon-like slab of a face and big hands. This one sported two guns, and a sombrero added inches to his already considerable height.

Further study revealed that each sported twin six-shooters and both carried rifles thrusting up from saddle scabbards.

Scouts, possibly, he mused. But what kind of scouts? And why up here?'

Morgan nodded to himself now as a sudden suspicion jolted him.

Vallinova!

His enemy was camped on his trail and he could envision him dispatching a pair of scouts like this to reconnoitre. But for the heavy blanket of snow the horsemen would have most likely ridden on down the trail to reach the ranch house. As it was, they likely didn't even yet realize they were on ranch land, for the Atlanta cattle were all being held in a deep protective canyon at the far end of the valley out of the weather.

A nerve began to pulse in Morgan's neck as he watched the pair drink steaming coffee from battered tin mugs. He'd all but convinced himself he'd shaken Vallinova down in Weeping Woman Valley, had even shrugged aside the late information that the Mexican killer had added a top trailsman to his bunch, the gringo Foley Haig.

Bitterness set in as he slowly fingered his hat back from his forehead and drew the back of his hand across his mouth.

He realized he'd deluded himself into believing he'd really lost them. Vallinova was rated as the most dangerous man on either side of the border and was about the last bastard you wanted camped on your trail. He'd heard it said the outlaw's only concession to humanity was the way he had idolized his kid brother.

Had done.

Blaze Morgan had killed Miguel Vallinova with two bullets to the head down in Yellow Gulch, Oklahoma, months earlier. Brother Juan had been camped on his trail ever since, vowing to stick to it until one of them was dead.

The last reliable information Morgan had had on the killer was that Vallinova had a bunch of his killers from Arizona riding with him — insurance to make doubly sure his brother's 'murderer' would pay out his blood debt.

Suddenly Morgan seemed overtaken by a terrible lethargy. He'd never wanted to slay Miguel Vallinova, son of Fifty-Peso Juanita, the raven-haired harlot queen of Sonora. But Miguel was dead and gone now and forgotten by most everybody with the exception of his brother . . . maybe the worst exception imaginable.

Although aware of the risk in just lying there within a stone's throw of the killers, still Morgan didn't move. *You killed and you killed and it never ended*, he thought bitterly. Why not get it over and done with now? Front Vallinova and settle the blood debt here and now . . . He straightened suddenly and the unsettling moment of weakness was gone, banished by an act of will. The killers were the reality and must be dealt with, and only he might accomplish it.

What must happen was suddenly crystal clear. Head back to the ranch house and warn the Garfields. If they moved fast the couple could likely get clear of the danger zone altogether. Likely they knew a secret way out of the valley which they could use. Hell, maybe they could all go together? He was not afraid of Vallinova, just of further slaughter. He craved peace, never more so than right at that moment . . .

Flight. Plainly the only solution that made sense.

Wriggling back from the rim of the low incline, he rose, only to step upon a frozen stick embedded in the snow. The stick cracked beneath his weight, the sound seeming shotgun-loud in the snowy stillness.

For a moment he seemed unable to move, but in the next instant his joints unlocked and he went streaking for his horse.

The head and shoulders of the smaller of the two gunmen hove into sight above the rim as Morgan vaulted up and over the appaloosa's hindquarters and hit leather. The outlaw had a gun in either hand as he filled his lungs to shout.

'Halt!' he roared. Then recognition hit. 'Morgan! *Sì* . . . it is Morgan — I kill!'

Morgan's draw was was lightning fast. The Navy Colt angled sharply across his body was spewing flame and thunder before the hellion could fire. He threw up both arms and dropped from sight, six-guns describing glittering arcs in the wintry sunlight before being engulfed by the snow.

The appaloosa whirled in response to Morgan's jerk on the reins, then leapt forward to the touch of spur.

Back in the hollow the smaller gunman

lay sprawled in death in blood-spattered snow while his partner heeled his mount upslope. This guntoter wasn't built for speed and had been delayed in running for his rifle. Yet he reached the crest with the fleeing Morgan still within range. Instantly dropping belly-flat he cuddled the smooth stock to his cheek, fixed the foresights upon Morgan's broad back and gently stroked trigger.

It was a good shot, almost a great one, considering the factors of distance and a moving target. The bullet slammed the cantle of Morgan's saddle and scorched a light hot furrow along his left thigh. He slewed the appaloosa right, then left as the rifle bellowed again. One slug slashed the snow off to his right and the next plopped harm-lessly behind.

He was suddenly out of range!

Above the grunting sounds of his mount, Morgan heard three shots in rapid suc-cession. A brief pause, then two more. But horse and rider remained unscathed. Hipping around in the saddle he glimpsed the powerful figure of the gunman stand-ing outlined against a snowy backdrop, methodically firing the Winchester into the sky.

Morgan realized he was signalling to Vallinova that they had found their man!

Morgan turned to the trail ahead and didn't look back. He could still hear the dimming voice of that rifle summoning Vallinova and his killers as he swept over the hill crest that brought the great house into sight.

* * *

Morgan's voice sounded hoarse, his breathing laboured. 'No other way out? There's got to be!'

Standing before the gunfighter in the front room of the great house with scissors in one hand and a bottle of raw spirits in the other, a strangely calm Luke Garfield shook his curly head.

'The only way in or out of the valley is by that trail up from Weeping Woman Valley, Mr Morgan. But forget that for now — let me see to that leg.'

Morgan's angry blow sent the bottle flying all the way across the room. 'The hell with my leg, it's only a goddamned crease! That'll be nothing compared to what we can expect if we don't get the hell out of here, fast!'

Morgan sounded fearful, and was. But not for himself. In this desperate hour he'd found himself suddenly feeling intensely protective towards the dead rancher's children. Responsible. And knowing who it was coming after him, knew he had good reason to feel that way.

Hannah crossed the room to retrieve the bottle. The girl wore the same infuriatingly composed expression as her brother as she passed the bottle to him.

'There is no place to go, Mr Morgan,' she said lifelessly. 'Perhaps we could hide . . . but the snow would betray us . . . '

Her words trailed off. She didn't have to explain to him that flight would be suicidal in these conditions. Not even the smallest of creatures could move through snow without leaving its tell-tale tracks, which any predator could follow — animal or human.

Morgan sucked in a huge breath. 'All right . . . all goddamn right!' he growled, and was suddenly calm. The wound, the headlong gallop to the house and the understanding of the situation had abraded his nerves. But only briefly. At such times he could always tap into a hidden reserve of strength such as was coursing through his veins right now. His one certainty was that even if Vallinova were to carry this hour, he would make sure it cost him dear.

He vowed not to die unless he took that murdering son of a bitch into the Big Dark with him!

His thoughts raced and his mind was suddenly crystal clear as he nodded to the youth.

'Luke, I want you to go saddle two mounts, one for you and one for your sister. This dog who wants to kill me has nothing against you. He'll let you quit the valley — it's just me he's after right now. So you go and keep on going . . . '

He broke off when he saw that the youth was shaking his head.

'This is our home, Mr Morgan. We won't leave it.'

This was the unexpected. Morgan had to fight to keep his temper. 'Goddamnit,' he snapped, gesturing at the windows. 'You don't understand. These aren't penny-ante hardcases like Greenberry or Foley out there. Vallinova is a killer who wants me dead and he'd wipe out half this county to see it. And you could bet your life he'd cut down anyone he caught with me — like you and your sister. Can't you get that through your head — either of you?'

He turned appealingly to the girl but found no help there. She was wearing the same inflexible expression as her brother.

'We must stay, Mr Morgan,' she said. 'Our home is all we have left in life now. We'll help you fight for it.'

He couldn't believe it. But instantly he realized he had no option. Plainly their unnatural lives here and their upbringing had shaped them into strange and different people. Yet even in that moment he was impressed, almost understanding. For this was all they had; what would they have were they to cut and run?

His mind was suddenly made up. They would not leave. So he could not leave them. Which left but the one course of action.

'Where are you going, Mr Morgan?' the girl asked as he fitted his hat to his head and made for the door.

'Leaving,' he stated flatly, pausing to check out his six-guns. 'I'll have it out with Vallinova away from here . . . which should give you some chance at least.'

'No!' Hannah gasped, horrified. 'That would be suicide. You must fight from here — we need you to stay here with us, not throw your life away for no reason.'

'Every reason,' he countered, and was reaching for the door handle when the girl began to weep. Her brother went to her side and held her, staring at Morgan over her head in a way that first caused him to halt, then drop his hand from the door.

They were right. He could not leave. Would not.

A gust of wind rattled the windows and when they looked out they saw them coming. Sharply etched against the snow, their dark and menacing silhouettes astride big horses with harnesses winking in the weak sun, came the Vallinova gang, riding boldly like the heroes of a battle already won.

7

Man from Sonora

Even back in Mexico, where hard men were unafraid to wear silver rings in their ears and frilled lace at wrist and throat, Juan Vallinova had stood out as flamboyant. Thirty years old and as lithely built as a matador, the Sonoran pistolero believed in few popular adages, but one he embraced fully was the one that proclaimed, 'Clothes maketh the man.'

'That Juan,' his late and unlamented brother Miguel had often boasted, 'I say he would rather be dead and dressed in fine linen than alive and healthy but condemned to rags. Is strange, no?'

Seated astride his tall white horse as he halted just beyond gun range of the great house in the valley, Vallinova still looked splendid despite the fact that he had been living in the open for more than a week as they camped on the trail of his brother's killer. Snug-fitting charro pants were clean, the waist-length leathern vest fitted his lean torso perfectly, and the black sombrero was brushed spotless — thanks to Slim Whitby whose task it was to ensure he always looked the part for the real life role he played with such zest and ferocity.

In contrast to his attire the bandido's gun rig was black and unadorned, just two plain six-guns in cutaway holsters, buckled low. While all else was show and vanity, the Colts were for the killing that was essential to maintain his legend and his power.

Like any newcomer to Atlanta Ranch, Vallinova was deeply impressed by his first sighting of the late Martha Henderson's mansion. Yet it was but a fleeting moment. The Mexican slaughterman's total focus that snowy morning was centred upon one thing and one only.

Revenge.

There was no sign of life at the house or its wide scatter of outbuildings and corrals, though there was a momentary glimpse of movement behind a high window. Several of the outsized front windows of the mansion were boarded up. The giant cottonwood at the far corner of the main building was now beginning to stir in a chill breeze. It was very quiet all across that shimmering mountain snowscape.

Vallinova hipped around and jerked his chin at the man astride the shaggy grey mustang directly behind. The rider immediately drew abreast, fringed buckskins causing a faint whispery sound, his shoulder-length hair streaming out behind like a woman's crowning glory.

Foley Haig was in high standing with the Sonoran desperado for it was Vallinova's gringo scout who was responsible for the gang being here within sniffing distance of Blaze Morgan in that snowy winter time.

Down in Weeping Woman Valley

several days earlier Morgan had done such a masterful job of blotting his tracks that even Haig, one-time army scout and mountain man, had found it impossible to pick up the trail. But while Vallinova raged and fumed, Foley was busy scouting mining trails, tote roads and the lower ranges until he'd cut a single hoofprint fifteen miles west of where they had lost Morgan's sign.

The indentation, frozen in place by frost, was immediately identified by Haig, who eventually realized it was imprinted upon a trail that led upwards into the higher country which nobody seemed to know much about. Vallinova headed up to the heights, a vital decision which had finally led them to where they were today, all thanks due to buckskinned Foley.

Valinova gestured at the mansion. 'Discover if Morgan is there, *amigo*.' He tapped the side of his nose with a forefinger. 'This tells me it is so . . . I scent his evil blood. But we must be sure.'

Haig threw a half-salute and hipped around in the saddle.

'Whitby, Dobbs and Flynn,' he ordered. 'Follow me!'

The three riders broke from the line and Haig led them away without delay. Fanning out like the professionals they were, the party began to circle the headquarters in search of something, anything, that might might point to Morgan still being there.

The hellions rode tense in the saddle and kept just beyond rifle range of the silent house. All Vallinova's men were dedicated killers who made few errors.

Their circling patrol of the headquarters was carried out without incident and Vallinova was puffing a thin black cigarillo with one polished boot cocked over the saddle horn when Haig and his men returned to report.

'No tracks leading out apart from them left by Morgan himself earlier, Juan.'

Vallinova nodded faintly, eyes distant and narrowing now. 'So . . . he is still there . . . '

He blew a smoke ring that was immediately snatched away by the breeze. After a moment, he began muttering, as if thinking out loud. 'It is plain that others are here besides Morgan . . . men who will likely risk their lives and die should gunplay break out. Yet Morgan is a hero, no?'

Realizing an answer was expected, Slim Whitby obliged, 'So it is said, Juan.'

Vallinova smiled. He was ready to grind that great house to rubble if needs be, yet was reluctant to risk valuable men. He sensed it would cost him dear if he had to smoke Morgan out. But maybe it could all be done without a single shot being fired? Had Morgan made a fatal error of judgement in returning to this place?

Without turning, he called, 'Henry!'

The outsized outlaw who had come so close to gunning Morgan down, came forward astride his ugly brown gelding. Shep Henry was in bad standing with the leader since Morgan had killed his saddle pard, Lang Short. The gunner had tried to convince him Short's death was unavoidable but the leader was unimpressed.

'Yes, sir, boss man?' Henry said eagerly, reining in. He was keen to erase the blot on his record.

'Go take a message to Morgan, Shep. Tell him if he quits the house now the people will be spared. If he doesn't agree, we kill them all, and him slowest of all.'

Henry gulped. 'You mean . . . I ride in there alone, Juan?'

Vallinova made no response but his expression spoke volumes. It proved eloquent enough to affect thick-witted Shep Henry, who straightaway turned his prad away, and heels slammed horsehide.

Watching the big rider recede through the drifts and clear patches, Foley Haig's edginess did not go unnoticed.

'You doubt my tactics, Foley?' Vallinova queried.

'Uh . . . well, no . . . sound enough I

guess. But this Morgan . . . '

His words trailed off. The leader's hawk features turned cold. 'Finish what you started, *amigo*. What about Morgan?'

'Well, we know he's just so damned dangerous, boss . . . '

His words trailed off, but had already done their damage. Vallinova was quietly enraged and offended by the general nervousness regarding Morgan, even if underneath he might agree the gunfighter warranted respect. A fast gun's vanity was always an edgy, touchy thing.

'I still believe that if Morgan has others with him at the house he will surrender rather than place them all at risk,' he said stiffly, then looked away.

His gunman had almost reached the house now and he felt his skin prickling with tension as he raked his gaze across the high windows and kept fingering the handle of his Peacemaker as the mansion loomed nearer.

Big Shep had grit, yet still took off his bandanna and waved it overhead — the universal invitation to parley. He reined his mount to a dead stop as the heavy, bullet-scarred front door of the mansion opened and Blaze Morgan emerged.

Morgan's hands were empty, a fact Shep Henry recognized as the gunfighter displaying contempt for an inferior.

Anger stirred in Henry's sluggish brain. The big man staring down at him had blasted his pard, Lang Short, reduced his status with Vallinova, and now seemed intent on lording it over him before the eyes of both friends and foes alike, as if he was holding all the cards.

'Morgan!'

'What is it, scum?'

The insult stung yet Henry managed to keep calm as he delivered Vallinova's ultimatum. Morgan heard him out in silence, staring across the broad expanse of white to the long crest where the outlaws were drawn up in line.

Then abruptly turning his back he vanished back inside, leaving Henry white with rage. This arrogant bastard was treating him like a farm boy!

An eerie quiet enveloped the scene. The hellions were edgy, had no way of knowing that, inside, Morgan was attempting to convince Luke and Hannah that Vallinova would likely leave them be should he turn himself over to the enemy. Brother and sister were shocked by the proposal, terrified for Morgan and themselves if the gunfighter should surrender. But to a realistic Morgan, calculating the uneven odds, it seemed like some slim chance for the young innocents at least, something they might well be denied should he decide to fight it out to the bitter end. Then the girl's voice lifted and Henry ground his teeth impotently when he heard her begging the gunfighter to stay with them and help them fight.

Silence fell again and Henry began to sweat. Glancing back he saw his support had moved back some distance. They could be readying to retreat if negotiations turned sour, leaving him isolated. His eyes played restlessly over the vacant windows again. There were no signs of life until, after what seemed an eternity, the gallery door creaked open again.

Morgan appeared paler as he emerged to cross the gallery with a slight limp. He halted with arms folded to focus on the distant Vallinova.

'No deal, scum!' he shouted, ignoring Henry.

Henry's pig eyes flared with resentment. 'You're a damn fool, Morgan! You'll all burn now and I'll dance on your lousy g — '

Vallinova yelled something back but nobody heard. Henry was raging now as Morgan turned away, heavy-shouldered and seemingly resigned to something he now felt powerless to change.

That did it.

Suddenly all rage and resentment, Henry cursed and clawed at the big gun riding his hip.

All he needed was one good shot.

Morgan was almost to the door when

143

Hannah Garfield's fearful look as she stared beyond him touched off the alarm bells. His response was electrifying. Twisting and coming clear in one explosive moment, he jerked trigger twice before Shep Henry could bring his Peacemaker up to firing level.

The first shot lifted Henry erect in his stirrups and the next blasted him out of the saddle. There was no pain for the victim, just a thudding shock as though someone had struck him twice with a powerful fist to the chest. He crashed to earth on his left side but didn't feel that either. The real pain was the realization Morgan had suckered him with that back-turning routine to tempt him into making a play — his final fool play.

Then he rolled on to his back and wondered, in his last moment this side of eternity, why the blue winter sky had suddenly turned black.

★ ★ ★

Drawing within gun range of the great house astride his racing pony, outlaw Elroy Dobbs slid from the saddle at full gallop on the blind side, Indian style, and fired at the rear windows from under the racing animal's belly.

His first two shots went high but the third whipped between Luke Garfield's body and arm just as the boy was about to fire the old-fashioned rifle. Luke flinched, but was still struggling to fix a bead on the chicken coop where Casey Flynn had taken cover, when Morgan came charging into the back room and slammed him away from the window with a shoulder charge.

'How many times do I have to tell you?' the gunfighter shouted above the stutter of gunfire. 'You load them and I'll fire them!'

Morgan's six-gun blasted at Dobbs's fast receding figure then Blaze spun to blast a bullet at the chicken coop. Next moment, the hammer clicked upon an empty chamber. Morgan ducked low as Vallinova's Winchester repeater chimed in to rake the wall above him with a vicious volley.

Gunsmoke was wreathing the room as Morgan bellied across the floor to reach the dazed Luke. He jerked the rifle from the boy's hands and replaced it with his empty Colt.

'Just load it, don't shoot!' he repeated. He started off for the hallway, paused. 'Didn't hurt you any, did I, kid?'

The boy shook his head. 'I'm fine, Mr Morgan. But you will have to let me back you up sooner or later. You can't stand them off on your own forever.'

'I've done all right so far,' Morgan retorted, checking the rifle's loads. He wasn't bragging, merely wanted to keep their confidence up as the gunplay intensified.

'But for you, Sis and me would have been done for long back,' the boy insisted, fingering fresh shells into the Colt from his pocket.

The gunfighter's jaw set hard. 'You shouldn't even damn well be here.'

Luke made no reply. They'd settled all of that earlier when Henry had ridden in to deliver Vallinova's terms. The siblings still feared and mistrusted Morgan, yet Vallinova's dog pack terrified them. Their choice had been either to remain with a man whom they at least knew a little, or to split from him and likely place themselves at the mercy of a man whom Morgan labelled a 'dirty butcher'.

They'd stayed with Morgan, who had no way of knowing whether Vallinova would keep his word not to harm the Garfields, or whether he might not just as readily kill the boy and turn the girl over to his killers.

A fresh storm of shots from the front brought Morgan up in a low crouch. As he snaked for the door, Luke called after him, 'Getting low on bullets, Mr Morgan!'

'Tell me something I don't know!' Morgan snapped back, and was gone, pounding headlong down the hallway just as the sounds of Dobbs's racing pony grew louder.

Gunsmoke writhed in tendrils around Morgan's big frame as he lunged into the tiny sewing room. Instantly, he sprang atop a low bench to reach a window. He made it just in time to jerk up his piece and blast away at the racing figure of the outlaw as he came storming past the hitchrack with his Colt belching flame and thunder from beneath his horse's neck.

There was no hope of striking the obscured Dobbs, but the paint pony made a big target. Morgan triggered twice and the animal went down on its nose and somersaulted end over end in a wild blur of threshing hoofs and flying snow.

The outlaw went sailing through space until striking the ground in a storm of profanity. Forced to expose himself by leaning from the window, Morgan was bringing gunsights to bear on the dazed hardcase when Foley Haig appeared around the south corner of the house and sent him diving for cover

148

beneath a vicious volley of six-gun lead.

Slumping against a wall with fragments of wood and glass spraying down upon him, Morgan realized he'd not been struck, couldn't quite figure why, shrugged and spun over to fast-crawl his way across the gloomy lobby to gain the parlour.

'Stay down!' he panted on sighting Hannah crouched by the cellar doorway beneath the stairs. Next instant he was gone, and soon the girl heard the crashing roar of his Colt as he settled down to a close-quarters duel with the buck-toothed hellion positioned in the back of the stone water trough.

And those guns did roar . . .

Although the death toll had not increased since Henry choked on blood, the situation for the defenders was deteriorating by the minute. It was impossible for Morgan to cover front and rear entrances successfully, even though his vicious fire power prevented the outlaws from staging a rush. But having full control of the outbuildings and all available cover, the killers were able to keep him on the move now, driving him from one spot to another, switching their attack unpredictably to run him ragged and help exhaust his ammunition.

Morgan knew this game. He'd played it himself. He let the boy reload for him but banned Hannah from taking any part. Tension heightened, the guns bellowed . . . and he kept counting how many bullets were left . . .

From time to time he heard Vallinova's loud voice bawling orders. That hellion knew the game he was playing, would counter him with equal skill . . . maybe even play his own game better . . .

Morgan blanked his mind. He went low then bobbed up momentarily to punch a shot into the wash room. Then came Hammah's involuntary cry as a wild bullet keyholed through wallboards somewhere close and clattered away noisily before silencing abruptly.

'Are you all right, Hannah?' he roared.

'Yes, Mr Morgan.'

'Stay down!'

'If you say so . . . '

Uncertain minutes passed for Hannah before she realized she'd not heard her brother's voice in some time. Defying Morgan's instructions she darted the length of the long hallway on flying feet to reach the rear room. She gasped in relief on sighting Luke standing by the bullet-ruined window clutching the big Richardson shotgun, staring out.

Luke shot her a weary grin as she entered then motioned for her to keep back from his window.

Suddenly he raised the weapon, but changed his mind and let it drop again. 'Could have got him, maybe,' he muttered. 'Can't afford to waste a single bullet now . . . '

'Mr Morgan said you were not to do any shooting, Lukey.'

The boy looked rueful. 'Don't fret. Nobody will be doing any shooting much longer, Sis.' He slapped his pockets. 'We're all but out of ammunition.' He hazarded a tired smile. 'Funny, but I never realized just how far it was from the house to the tack room until today.'

The girl knew what he meant. Their father had always insisted they store all dangerous materials such as coal-oil, poisons and ammunition well away from the mansion out in the little tack-room. There were several cases of bullets and shotgun shells out there beneath a pile of sacks upon the workbench. It was barely eighty feet from the rear of the mansion, but this was now a murderous eighty feet of no man's land.

Hannah drew closer to her brother and he put his arms about her shoulders. They stood thus together in silence listening to the deep-throated roar of the shooting from out front, drawing strength and comfort from each other as they'd done so often in the past. Mystery, violence and disaster seemed part of this strange lost place they called home, yet it seemed they would always be safe just so long as they had one another.

The room began to grow gloomy with approaching dusk. The hellions for now appeared content to maintain their positions and keep sniping from cover. Slim Whitby stoically continued to hold his defensive post out front behind the water trough, while Casey Flynn and the unhorsed Elroy Dobbs were stationed at the stables where the outlaws had earlier been surprised to find four cold corpses maintaining a graveyard vigil in the horse stall.

The sturdy cattle sluice out by the title gate provided Vallinova with security and comfort along with his slim black cigars, his walnut-handled six-guns and the belief that time was on his side.

Eventually Luke left his sister to go through to the front with freshly loaded guns for Morgan. He would deliver as well the grim information that when these guns were emptied Atlanta Ranch would be out of ammunition and defenceless against their enemies.

Moving to the corner of the great room that was ornamented by oil paintings of her parents in their great days before everything went so tragically wrong, Hannah absorbed the scents and sounds of the great house, stood listening to the murmur of the male voices. She could identify the different voices but their words were a blur. And yet she could tell that Morgan sounded confident and reassuring, even though she knew even he must realize it was now but a matter of time.

Somehow she couldn't stop herself thinking just how different it could all be if only those many boxes of shells weren't sitting out there . . . so near and yet so far . . .

8

Siege Guns

Foley Haig grunted as he mounted up and circled around to Vallinova's position in the gathering dusk, making certain he kept well out of gun range and keeping the chicken coop as cover.

The Mexican shootist turned to stare at him as he swung down, then returned his gaze to the mansion. 'So?' Vallinova's voice was soft yet sharp.

'So? So . . . what's the plan then, Juan?'

Vallinova smiled mockingly. 'So impatient, eh, *amigo*? Do you know that more pistoleros have perished from impatience than from all the bullets of their enemies — ' He broke off on noticing Haig's blood-stained shoulder. 'You have been hit?' he frowned.

'Just a crease,' Haig answered, flexing

his arm. 'Lucky it's the left wing . . . '
His voice faded and he frowned
pensively. 'Those sons of whores throw
mean lead, boss man.'

'They save their best work for
murdering boys!'

Haig forgot his shoulder as he met
Vallinova's suddenly bleak eye. The
gringo killers in this wolf pack had
always been puzzled by the leader's
high regard for his kid brother, the 'boy'
to whom Vallinova was now alluding.
Their leader had always regarded the
younger Vallinova as a cross between El
Cid and the Angel Gabriel, while to
hardbitten gunners like Foley Haig he'd
been just a foul-tempered little wetback
always destined to die young and badly.

He and the others had secretly
celebrated when Miguel was chopped
to ribbons in a murderous gun battle at
Yellow Gulch, while killer Vallinova had
wept like a bereaved bride.

Juan's feelings for his kinsman went
a long way back. The two brothers were
born and reared in a bordello, a fact

that Juan's legions of enemies never allowed him to forget. As soon as he was as mature and lethal as any grown man, at age eleven, Juan Vallinova said goodbye to the mother, Fifty-Peso Juanita, the Jewel of Sonora, and set out to carve his name in borderland history with a Colt .45.

He succeeded bloodily and money, fame and women were all his long before maturity. Yet Vallinova always felt keenly his lack of class and background and, as big-breasted Juanita was quite beyond the pale in every way that counted, he concentrated his attentions on Miguel.

He took him under his wing, taught him all the finer points of killing people and boasted to the world of his brother's prowess, predicting that one day the world would tremble at the very name of the Brothers Vallinova.

Side by side, Juan and Miguel Vallinova would carve their names with pride in the gunsmoke legends of the south-west and in so doing would eventually erase the stigma of being born the sons of a harlot.

So much for blind ambition.

The young Miguel who could never distinguish a class gunman from a tenth-rater, had decided to add Blaze Morgan's scalp to his belt. As a consequence he now lay stiff and stark in Yellow Gulch's Boot Hill, leaving his brother with the sacred responsibility of avenging his death.

Vallinova placed his cigar between his lips and drew deeply. As he exhaled luxuriously Foley saw that crazy, mean look fade from his eyes and realized it was safe to talk again.

'Do we plan to rush him at dark, Juan?'

'Perhaps.'

Haig frowned. 'But surely that'd be the best time, wouldn't it?'

Vallinova blew a perfect smoke ring. 'Do you observe that Morgan does not shoot so often as before, *amigo?*'

'Why, reckon as how I have.'

'There can be but one reason for this.

He runs low on shells. In time he will have none. *Then* we destroy him — and I shall drink his blood!'

Haig ran a finger around his shirt collar and nodded in uneasy agreement before the rear door of the great house eased slowly open. Tapping his leader and pointing, Haig lifted his rifle. The two watched, motionless, and after a minute saw the shadowy figure come creeping out through the doorway.

'Easy pickings,' grunted Haig, taking aim.

'Hold your fire!' Vallinova snapped. 'You see . . . it is not Morgan!'

'You must see in the dark much sharper than me, *amigo*,' Haig muttered, squinting hard. Then his eyes snapped wide. 'Well, I'll be damned! It's a gal!'

★   ★   ★

'Just show yourself another inch, butcher boy!' Morgan breathed softly over his gunsight. But buck-toothed badman Slim Whitby was suddenly behaving as though he suspected something, and didn't move one inch further over there by the meat house. Moments later he disappeared altogether as if scenting the mortal danger which he'd been in for just a moment or two.

Morgan cursed and lowered the gun. Squatting on the floor close by, fair hair bright in the fading light, young Luke Garfield studied him before speaking. 'You reckon they might all rush us come dark, Mr Morgan?' The boy's tone was calm and normal. Both brother and sister had dropped that monotone style of speaking during the siege, which Morgan regarded as something on the positive side. There were precious few other such signs tonight.

'I would if I was Vallinova,' he grunted.

A pause, then, 'It's too bad about the ammunition. If we'd only had a little more time before they came in . . . '

Morgan nodded in silence, still focused on Whitby's position.

The Garfields had not informed him

about the ammunition store until too late. He'd briefly considered the possibility of making a dash for the tack room and the ammunition once it was dark but doubted he would attempt it now.

He figured the enemy would start closing in with the full onset of night, and so considered his prospects of getting to the tack room, collecting the ammunition, then making it safely back to the house, as murderously slender.

Alone, he reckoned he might have taken that chance. But he was anything but that. He had two young people dependent upon him for their very survival and, regardless of the fact that they'd tried to kill him and lied to him at every turn, he still felt full responsibility for the pair. He was constantly aware that, but for his coming here in the first place the youngsters would not be in the desperate situation they surely were now.

He let out a weary gust of breath and watched the last traces of crimson fade from the low clouds rimming the eastern skyline.

It seemed odd, he mused, that the mystery of Atlanta Ranch and its two strange, young inhabitants had barely enterered his mind that day. From the moment he'd first cut that sign out at the northern end of the valley his mind had been occupied with but one hope. Survival. And with every passing minute drawing nightfall nearer now he knew that hope had to be diminishing.

Vallinova had numbers, ammunition and descending nightfall as allies. He had all the odds, and Morgan sighed, bitterly regretting he had been unable to trim the enemy ranks even further than he had. Big Shep Henry and runty Lang Short had been valuable scalps. But the enemy was still at least five strong, and each of those five had proven himself that long afternoon.

Abruptly he jerked alert.

Whitby was on the move again!

Morgan knew the outlaw must be experiencing the effects of cramp now that the cold was biting deeper. Intent, motionless, Morgan watched one long leg stretch out slowly, flex, disappear, then the other. Realizing his man was making ready to reveal himself, Morgan cocked his Colt .45 again and held his body low, still as death. Waiting. If that buck-tooth butcher showed as much as an eyebrow he would drill him dead centre!

A scream rose from someplace in back.

'Hannah!' Luke groaned, and leaping erect, led the way from the room at a run.

The first thing Morgan noted as he stormed into the hallway in pursuit was the rear door standing ajar. Drawing abreast of Luke, he seized him by one arm, reeled him back then swung him through the doorway without breaking his own stride.

He skidded sideways to a halt in the doorway just in time to glimpse a wildly struggling Hannah Garfield disappearing beyond the tack room door in the brutal arms of Foley Haig.

Morgan didn't hesitate. 'Cover me, kid!' he bawled back to an invisible Luke then leapt through the doorway.

His sheer explosiveness took Vallinova by surprise just after the killer seized the initiative by sending Haig into the tack room after the girl. His plan had been to seize Hannah and hold her in the tack room until full dark when it would be safe to move her further away from the house where they would be free to torture her and do whatever they pleased until Morgan was forced to surrender.

But Vallinova had had no time to organize the rest of his bunch as yet and, as a result, he suddenly found himself the only man within gun range as Morgan erupted into sight.

'*Amigos*! To the rear!' he bawled, then triggered.

The slug clipped Morgan's shirt collar as he launched his body into an immense curving dive which saw him strike ground ten feet ahead and kick himself out through the arched doorway.

A six-gun roared.

He ignored it as he hurtled down a short hallway and was suddenly outside! Rolling and kicking his way erect Morgan heard Vallinova screaming in Spanish and he began zig-zagging across open space for the tack room where the girl was being held.

As he rushed onwards he realized Vallinova was circling at incredible speed around the yard and would surely beat him to that doorway now.

Only one thing for it. Forget the door and take the shorter route to the window! Closing in on the building, Morgan found he could dimly make out the twisting, struggling figures within. Then he saw that the side window, though small, was maybe just about big enough . . .

Without hesitation he crossed both arms in front of his face, bunched powerful thigh muscles then threw himself at the window like a battering ram.

Haig's first warning was the explosion of glass and, before he could react, 180 lb of gunfighter crashed his way through into the tiny room, knocking both girl and outlaw to the floor.

Shedding glass and debris Morgan thudded into the floor hard, yet was still first to regain his feet. He flinched instinctively as a bullet from Vallinova's storming Colt whined desperately close, then leapt clear of the opening as a snarling Haig shook himself free of entanglement with the girl and made it to his feet.

Their six-guns were almost touching as Morgan jerked trigger, drilling a .45 slug through Foley Haig's windpipe and shattering his backbone.

It wasn't a good way to die and Haig was dying hard, choking and twisting like a sinner in torment upon the bloodied floor.

Morgan had no time to administer the mercy shot. Right now life could be measured in moments. Heeling the door shut a split second before

Vallinova's shoulder crashed into it with a force that shook the whole building, he scooped up the dazed girl in his arms, jumped across Haig's agonized form then heaved her bodily out through the window, jagged glass ripping his forearm.

'Run!' he roared as she dropped from sight, then spun back for the door. He reefed it open and caught Vallinova off guard as he wildly beckoned to Casey Flynn who came running up from the stables.

Morgan triggered twice. But Vallinova was no longer there. Displaying his astonishing reflexive speed, the killer had hurled his lithe body headlong to the right and disappeared behind a half-door.

It was a costly miss for him, Morgan knew. Yet it forced Vallinova to kick frantically to gain more solid cover, and so was unable to return Morgan's fire for the moment for fear of exposing himself.

Slamming the battered door shut

again, Morgan whirled away and, as he clambered atop the bench by the window, he glimpsed the ammunition boxes which Hannah had collected prior to Haig coming through the door behind her. Shoving the gun into his belt, he snatched up the boxes then hurled himself out the way he'd come in — through the window.

Hannah Garfield had by this time already gained the sanctuary of the house's rear door when Morgan come nosediving through the shattered window of the tack room to land heavily on one shoulder, roll violently behind the cover of a trace box then lie breathless.

He had no way of knowing that Hannah had gained the house safely despite being fired upon by Flynn from the wash house. And while Dobbs was out of gun range at the stables, Slim Whitby had paused to take stock of the gunplay from the north corner of the mansion.

Flynn didn't give a damn about failing to shoot the girl down. But

Morgan was a different matter. As the big gunfighter had dived through the window, hit hard, rolled and came up on one knee clutching his shoulder, the running Flynn was slamming on the brakes, sliding in slushy snow as he whipped up his .45 to firing level.

His attention now focused upon the mansion, Morgan failed to sight Flynn. But Luke Garfield did. The youth suddenly opened up from his window with the rifle. His aim was none too good but the thunder of the weapon caused Flynn to jerk trigger too fast with the result that he missed his intended target by a solid yard.

Grim-faced and still kneeling Morgan fired across his body, the shot spilling its flame like a venomous flower in the deepening gloom. The shot was marginally wide but caused Flynn to slew defensively sideways as he readied to shoot again. The gunner's crabwise movement coincided with Luke Garfield's next deliberate shot from the window. The soft-nosed .38 slug caromed off the chamber of Flynn's Colt, ricochetted upwards and struck him under the jaw, tore through his mouth and embedded in his brain.

He fell like a stone and never moved again.

Morgan saw Flynn fall but next moment was rolling violently himself as hot lead came his way from the lanky Slim Whitby who was readying to shoot again from the corner of the house. Desperately, Morgan fired back and Whitby ducked from sight moments before Hannah reached Morgan's side, grabbing him by the arm and helping him to his feet.

'Little fool!' he gasped, but didn't mean it. Holding hands, they ran for the house in the near dark, expecting bullets that failed to come. Up ahead, Luke was in the doorway urging them on, and then they were up the steps and diving for safety and knew they'd made it only when the youth slammed the door shut behind them.

Bullets thudded home but that good

door held secure and Morgan was astonished to find he was in one piece and seemed to be smiling. Next thing he knew he was slipping into darkness.

* * *

Morgan awoke to a pounding head and the taste of brandy on his lips. He shook his head, opened his eyes and sat up instantly.

'Vallinova!' he gasped. 'Where's my gun? What . . . ?'

A pale face swam before him, finally jumping into focus. The girl. He blinked. He realized they were in the big, old front room. It was almost dark. Suddenly the room shook to the deep-throated roar of a shotgun and by its vivid light he saw Luke's slim body outlined at the window.

'Are you all right, Mr Morgan?' Hannah's voice was uneven.

He clapped a hand to the back of his head and winced. His fingers came away sticky. Only now did he recall a sudden pain grabbing him during the run-in. He realized he must have been creased but didn't really know it at the time. As near as he could tell the slug must have scored the base of his skull at the hairline. He was nursing a headache, but was still very much alive, which made another one he owed Lady Luck.

'I'm fine,' he insisted, struggled to his feet and found himself able to straighten fully, if slightly unsteadily.

'Take a rest, Mr Morgan,' Luke insisted. 'They're scarce shooting at all now. I think we've about got them whipped.'

Morgan was none too certain about that. But if there was a lull in the fighting he knew he should make the most of it. Jerking out a chair, he dropped into it and was feeling about for something to wrap around his head when he belatedly remembered that Hannah had also been hit. Instantly, he rose and went to the girl as she bent to soak a bloodied cloth in a pitcher of water.

'Never mind that,' he said, taking the cloth from her hand. 'You've played nursemaid long enough. Now turn around and let me see your back.'

'No, Mr Morgan. It's just a scratch.'

'What?' Luke called in alarm. 'Is she hurt, Mr Morgan?'

'It's really nothing, Lukey,' Hannah insisted.

'Stop playing heroine,' Morgan said roughly, forcing her to turn about. He touched her back and felt blood, but couldn't tell if she was seriously hurt. He tapped her shoulder. 'Take off your blouse.'

'I'm all right — ' she began, but her brother cut her off.

'For heaven's sake, do as he says, Hannah!'

'But, Lukey, I — '

'No arguments, damnit!'

With a sigh, the girl took a deep breath and undid the buttons on her blouse. Morgan slipped the garment from her shoulders and reached for his matches. The brief spurt of flame showed him the girl's back clearly as he breathed, 'Good God!'

'Is it bad, Mr Morgan?' Luke cried in alarm.

'Hardly more than a light burn,' Morgan replied.

'Then why'd you take on that way?' the boy said touchily.

'You should know why, Lukey,' Hannah said with a strange calm. 'May I put my blouse back on now, Mr Morgan?'

'No, I'll clean you up first,' Morgan said. He immediately set to work gently and the girl didn't move. After sponging the burn clean, he then fetched a brandy bottle, warned it could hurt, applied the spirit generously. He could feel her tremble but she didn't cry out.

Luke fired at something at that moment and by the gunflash Morgan saw the girl's back clearly for a second time, confirming that what he'd seen first time was only too real. From waistline to shoulder, Hannah Garfield's back was a criss-cross of old scars. The only time Blaze Morgan had seen a back like that was during the dying days of the South, when slaves had shown their whipped bodies.

Morgan's voice sounded a little hoarse as he spoke. 'You can put your top back on now.'

Hannah drew the blouse over her shoulders and breasts then turned to face him as she did up the buttons. 'I can see you're shocked, Mr Morgan,' she said quietly, 'but it's nothing for you to worry about.'

'Who whipped you?'

To his astonishment, she smiled in the gloom of the big room and reached out to touch his hand. 'You saved my life at risk of your own, Mr Morgan,' she said wonderingly. 'Why did you do that?'

'Don't change the subject. How did you come by those scars?'

A rifle crashed somewhere, another answered. Then it was quiet again.

'How?' Morgan was relentless.

The girl's smile turned tremulous

and he caught the glint of tears in her eyes now. Her chin sank to her breast and the gunfighter reached out and drew her against him. She was so small, little more than a child. Yet God alone knew what she had had to endure in her young life.

'It's all right,' he reassured. 'Everything will be all right, you'll see.'

'Why did you save me?' she asked in a muffled voice. 'We were against you, yet you almost got killed saving me. Why?'

'Well, you were brave enough to go after that ammunition, even if it was a damn fool thing to do. And we need all the brave girls we can get.'

He realized he was speaking to her as if she was a child, which was seriously underrating her. She was plainly a woman with a woman's courage.

'We were cruel to you, yet you have been kind to us.' She spoke wonderingly, breaking away now to dab at her eyes. 'No-nobody has ever been kind to Lukey and me. Nobody . . . '

Before Morgan could respond, Luke called out. 'They're not shooting at all now, Mr Morgan. Maybe I'd better take a look out back.'

'I'll do it,' Morgan said sharply. He patted the girl's shoulder reassuringly, then turned away.

The shells were on the table.

Morgan scooped up a box and began fingering cartridges into his Navy Colt as he headed off down the corridor, mind racing, every sense acutely alert.

Hannah's sortie to the tack room had been as hair-raising a few minutes as he ever hoped to live through, he reflected, yet it had only improved their situation a little. Vallinova had lost two gunmen while the defenders had acquired enough ammunition to fight on for quite some time yet. They weren't in great shape maybe, but he knew it could easily have been a hell of a lot worse.

From a darkened window recess Morgan peered out warily. The stars were shining and the snow gleamed white. The enemy was no longer visible . . . no stir of movement in this unnaturally quiet night.

He raised his Colt deliberately and blasted a shot across the chicken coop, the echoes rolling away into the mountains, muttering.

Instantly, an answering shot came from the smithy. Morgan bobbed low, came up, touched off a shot towards the gunflash. He heard lead ricochet off metal and grimaced. Sounded as though he'd just drilled a blacksmith's anvil.

Then a voice hollered, 'That's gotta be Morgan, Juan! That kid can't shoot like that!'

A gun flared from the deeply recessed window of the meat house and Morgan was diving low again under a spray of wood fragments. An outlaw had just identified him by his gunplay and now, by the same yardstick, Morgan was sure that shooter at the meat house was Vallinova.

'Ho, greaser!' he shouted, refilling the six-gun.

'I hear you, Morgan!' The reply,

plainly from Vallinova, came from the meat house.

'You're not doing so well, greaser. You started off with six scum dogs at your heels, now you're down to three. If I was wearing your whorehouse boots I'd be feeling like a loser!'

The response was a storm of angry shots from the meat house which engulfed his voice as, hunkering low, Morgan grinned to himself. Vallinova was biting. If he could taunt him into something foolish or reckless he might yet carry the day.

Waiting for the gun echoes to fade away, Morgan filled his lungs and hollered again: 'What set you off this time, greaser? The part about the whorehouse? Hell, man, I wouldn't be sensitive about a little thing like that. I mean, there must be hundreds like you whose mothers run bordellos. And mighty few as handsome as Juanita, I'll wager.'

It was a long time before Vallinova replied. When he did, his voice was laced with controlled venom.

'Your voice issues from the grave, gringo. If you know how to pray, you should pray that I do not take you alive.'

Easing up and keeping well back from the window, Morgan rested his gun barrel across his left forearm, took a careful sighting on the meat house window, then emptied the weapon in one continuous rolling roar. The sixth shot was no sooner spent than Vallinova's six-gun roared thunderously and a startled Morgan felt the hot airwhip of the bullet's close passage by his right ear as he dived to the floor.

Morgan breathed hard. He'd needed that reminder, he told himself. Momentarily, he was forgetting he was up against one of the deadliest gunfighters ever seen in Juan Vallinova. It would be suicidal to underestimate him. This fight was a long way from being over.

Minutes ticked by. There was no further gunplay. There was no sound at all now except the whisper of the icy wind beneath the eaves of the great house.

9

Orphans of the Storm

The canyon slowly opened up before them as the lawmen's party halted on the high rim to stare off across the snow-flecked ridges to the mountain peaks high above.

The marshals from Wichita turned up their jacket collars and looked enquiringly at the sheriff.

Sheriff St John of Mission Fork was a blocky, brisk man with bright hazel eyes set in a high-coloured face. He was dressed plainly but well with his star pinned prominently on the slicker he wore over buckskin pants and jacket.

'Nothin' up thataway except more snow and ice than you fellers are likely to see from one year's end to another back in Wichita,' he told them.

'No trails at all?' queried Marshal Buck Reece.

'None.'

Reece was a large, dour man who'd first had the idea of tracking Blaze Morgan after news of Miguel Vallinova's death reached the marshal's office in Wichita.

The law had no warrant out on Morgan — indeed most peace officers would jump at the chance to shake the hand of the man who had rid them of Miguel Vallinova.

But Reece had a powerul hunch that Vallinova's lethal brother was certain to go after Morgan to avenge his sibling, and Juan had been a thorn in the side of the law these many years.

Reece wanted Vallinova badly and had been able to persuade his superiors to assign him and Doff Carter the task of tracking Morgan down in the hope that this in turn might lead them to Vallinova.

'Just a couple of goat tracks up there,' declared the Mission Fork lawman, who had been searching for a sign with the marshals over two long days ever since the snow had blotted out all sign of the Vallinova bunch in Weeping Woman Valley. The sheriff gazed wistfully southwards in the direction of Mission Fork. He shivered. 'Wouldn't be worth the ride up there as I see it.'

'We'll go take a look,' countered Reece, and both St John and Carter groaned inwardly. It was cold enough to make a man forget his religion up here, and the thermometer was certain to plunge even lower before daylight.

Reluctantly, St John turned his horse to lead the way upwards, following the switchbacks of a snake-like trail which clung precariously to the almost sheer face of the rock walls above the deep canyon.

The wind was cold up here, knifing down from the peaks and constantly threatening to blow men and horses down into the canyon on every sharp turn. Yet somehow all survived the climb, and then the travelling grew easier as they pushed on through ghostly pine forests and skirted the deep drifts.

It was almost midnight when they reached the tiny bridge over a foaming stream and continued to follow the dim track beyond to come eventually to the high bend in the trail where the wind had blown away the snow.

The prints of several horses in the soft earth were not fresh but were still plain to the eyes of the men who had been searching for them dilligently for several days.

It didn't take them long to be convinced that the tracks had to be those of the Vallinova gang, and even the dour Reece was looking more cheerful as he stared up the steeply climbing trail.

'What's up there, Sheriff?' he enquired.

'Just one outfit, about ten miles up,' supplied St John. 'Atlanta Ranch.'

'We'll take a look,' the marshal said and kicked his horse away. St John sighed as he set off after him. Earlier that week the sheriff had spent two fruitless days in the saddle hunting the desperadoes who had robbed the Mission Fork bank. He had a hunch this night ride to the Atlanta Ranch would prove to be just as much another wild goose chase as that had been.

* * *

The attack had lasted from midnight until after two o'clock. There were no casualties as far as Morgan knew, but fighting the outlaws off had cost him dearly in ammunition and energy.

Vallinova was plainly intent on wearing them down. He felt certain of this by the time he sat by the front window with a blanket wrapped around his shoulders staring out into the night. He had a hunch that the Mexican was planning to soften them up before launching his major assault. If that was how it happened then the defence would be ready.

It would have to be . . .

The coffee Hannah brewed and

brought across to him was just right . . . strong and black. Leaning back against the wall where he could keep one eye on the outside, he drank deep and waited for the good warmth to spread through his belly.

The girl took a cup across to her brother who was keeping watch out back, then returned to the main room.

'Lukey says everything is quiet out back, Mr Morgan,' she reported, going to the stove to pour her own coffee. Both the girl and her brother put a different inflection on his name now, Morgan had noticed, warm and trusting.

'This is good,' he murmured, closing his eyes for a brief moment. 'Real good.'

She peered across at him through the gloom. 'Won't you let me keep watch for a while so you can rest?'

'Nope.' He smiled as he tapped his forehead. 'This hard head is designed for bullets to bounce off should I get careless or sleepy, missy. Yours isn't. But you can talk to me if you want to help. That would help keep me sharp.'

She drew closer to take a seat at the end of the table. 'What would you like to talk about?'

'Isn't it about time you told me about you and Luke?'

For a long time there was no sound but the rising moan of the wind and the creaking of old timbers. Hannah Garfield stared down at her cupped hands as though they held some secret or mystery before turning to face him directly.

By the dim glow from the stove, the girl's pale, wide-eyed face showed a mixture of pain and resignation. 'It's not a pretty story, Mr Morgan. And you may not even believe it.'

'I'd still like to hear it. You've nothing to lose by telling me now, Hannah.'

'Why do you say that? Is it because you don't expect us to survive?'

'We *will* survive — no risk. No, it's on account I know about your father and that money . . . and also because

I'm hoping you can trust me now.'

The girl suddenly seemed too weary to resist and, turning in profile, quietly launched into a story which even Blaze Morgan might have found hard to believe had he not already known as much as he did about Atlanta Ranch by this time.

It was a tale of cruelty, terror and violent death which had its beginnings years earlier when the two children, living on a remote Colorado ranch with their parents, had lost their mother to the fever. She had been a weak and sickly woman, but kind and loving, in sharp contrast to her drunken brute of a spouse. Following the mother's death, there was nobody left to check Jesse Garfield's worst excesses. He took to beating his son and daughter on the slightest pretext, sometimes with fists or a strap, later with a whip. Their home was remote from neighbours; they were too terrified of the father to report him to the law.

Often leaving the children to work

the ranch, Garfield drank heavily, mixed with bad company and was bankrupt and just a short step from jail when their grandmother died and left them the Atlanta in her will.

Things improved for brother and sister for a time after their arrival here, Hannah conceded. But soon the old habits resurfaced. The father might be absent for days on end, during which periods she and Luke were expected to run the spread. When he returned, always in evil mood and hungover from liquor, he would take down the whip and use it on them. Things got so bad they were even punished for using the wrong inflection in their voices, and so they had developed that toneless manner of speaking which Morgan had initially found so strange.

The children had never visited Mission Fork. The father treated them like chattels and kept them hidden away in the mountains, slaving from daylight to dark with nobody to turn to but one another.

Then came the robbery.

Hannah and Luke had suspected something was afoot when outlaw Chip Greenberry visited their father on the Atlanta several times. Yet they had no notion what might be afoot until Jesse and Greenberry returned to the spread one night later, drunk and exuberant and tossing bundles of money into the air.

The two had robbed the Mission Fork bank.

But they'd staged the job without including Greenberry's owlhoot henchmen, Foley and Carney, which resulted in that pair eventually coming to search for them — and the money!

The robbery netted far more than expected, and so the two planned to head for Mexico to live like kings. But he wouldn't be taking anybody with them, Jesse had announced; Hannah and Luke could do as they pleased from here on in.

It was here that the story took a strange turn. Although living in terror of their brutal father, he was all the children had in life. His dictatorial domination ensured they had no outside contacts, friends or advisers. It was due to this abnormal environment that the two had come to fear the unknown outside world even more than their father and his cruelty. The bitter reality was that Jesse was all they had in life.

They agreed to do the only thing possible. They begged the father to stay, either that or take them along when he left.

Their pleas fell on deaf ears. He even appeared to enjoy their tears and terror which prompted his taunt that they were, 'Just as weak and dimwitted as your ma.'

That was when loyal Hannah slapped his face. Jesse seized the girl and began strangling her in his drunken fury. Luke called upon him to quit, but was ignored. Hannah's face was turning purple by the time a frantic Luke grabbed down the old rifle and drilled a four-ounce bullet through his father's heart and out his backbone . . .

An emotional Hannah was forced to break off her story here. Morgan waited patiently. At length she raised her head, sniffed once and continued.

With Jesse now dead they had disarmed the sodden Greenberry then locked him in the cellar, not wishing to kill the man yet afraid to release him.

It was but a short time later when Blaze Morgan had arrived and they suspected him to be either a friend of Jesse's, or the law. Either way, they decided, he also had to die. Yet when the time came they found the cold-blooded murder of a man who had done them no harm totally beyond them. Hannah eventually confessed to Morgan that they had stood at the foot of his bed for fully five minutes with the shotgun in hand before he awakened.

They later wept with relief that they hadn't killed him, even though fear and mistrust were naturally still present.

Try as he might, he'd been unable to

counter that mistrust until he'd saved Hannah's life. 'After that we knew we had been wrong about you, Mr Morgan,' the girl concluded tearfully. 'It was then we realized you were really a good man.'

Morgan sat staring at the coals, his expression deeply reflective in the dim glow of the stove. He was matching up what the girl had said with what he already knew and it all tallied. There was the ineffectual yet desperate way brother and sister had gone about trying to kill him ... how Jesse Garfield's features were stamped by cruelty and degeneracy even in death ... Greenberry imprisoned ... the subsequent arrival of Foley and Carney in search of their outlaw partner who had cut them out of the bank job ... the telling factor that the bank money was all here intact ...

He nodded slowly. He couldn't fault any of it now. But the crowning element had to be the simple fact that he felt he'd detected the sure ring of truth in every word the girl had uttered.

A strange story, he mused; sad, cruel and tragic. And, of course, a long way from finished as yet.

After a time, the girl spoke softly, 'Do you believe me, Mr Morgan?'

'I do, Hannah,' he replied, and didn't even hesitate.

'We-we did a terrible thing, didn't we?'

'I reckon that's not for me to judge.'

She turned away. 'If we all live through this, will you turn us in to the law?'

That was a tough question for Blaze Morgan to answer, a question that set up an inner conflict. There was compassion in the gunfighter that few people ever got to see and a part of him felt acutely for everything this boy and girl had suffered. Yet he was also a man with a high regard for justice and knew he was now burdened by the knowledge of how Jesse Garfield had died.

'Mr Morgan? Will you hand us over to the law?'

He shrugged and rose. 'I don't know Hannah . . . I just don't know . . . '

Hannah nodded as though understanding his dilemma. Then she said quietly, 'I'm not sorry for what we did. Our father was a terrible man and I'm glad he is dead. And no matter what happens, I still have Lukey.'

'Yeah, reckon you have at that.'

'But what about you, Mr Morgan? Don't you have anybody?'

He half smiled. 'Hey, you're getting this wrong, Miss Hannah. I hear confessions, I don't make them.'

'Then you have nobody in the whole world?' she pressed.

'Nobody — ' he began, then broke off. He was suddenly realizing that he uncharacteristically wanted to confide in this girl who, though little more than a child herself, seemed to have so much of a woman's wisdom and understanding.

So he rested a hand on the table corner, twisted a Bull Durham cigarette one-handed, and was soon talking freely about Grace Perrell, their memorable winter in fabled Denver — their love for one another . . . the break-up. He went on further than he had ever gone with anybody in telling this girl of his gunfighter's life, of his many attempts to change, of his failure.

He spoke of the men who had shadowed his steps, the vengeance seekers, the glory hunters . . . the Vallinovas. He even revealed how for a brief time he imagined he might have at last found a hidden sanctuary away from the world of blazing Colts and tombstones up here in the Flintlock Mountains.

And Hannah Garfield listened attentively to every word and even gave the impression she appeared to understand it all.

'Poor Mr Morgan. How lonely you are . . . just like us.'

The gunfighter's features hardened as he slid off the table. He could take just about anything from anybody but not sympathy.

'Too much talk is always worse than not enough, my father used to say,' he said gruffly. 'Would that coffee still be hot?'

'I'll go see,' Hannah smiled, as though she didn't take his gruffness seriously. But as she started for the stove they heard quick steps in the hall and moments later Luke stood framed in the doorway.

'Better come quick, Mr Morgan,' he panted. 'I reckon they're getting ready to start something again.'

Morgan stepped swiftly past the boy, then halted. 'You keep an eye on the front, son. And just remember, if anything should happen to me, you look out for your sister first and worry about yourself second. Hear?'

Luke appeared puzzled as he nodded, was still frowning as Morgan hurried off. 'A strange man, Sis,' he observed, moving to the window. 'One minute acting tough, the next fussing over us almost like Ma did. He's a hard man to understand, right enough.'

Hannah just smiled, for she felt she knew big Blaze Morgan very well by this time. And understanding the lonely man of the gun and having come to care for him, she prayed God wouldn't permit that Mexican outlaw to kill him. Yet the sudden eruption of gunfire from the rear told her that right at that moment Juan Vallinova might well be attempting to do just that.

10

Mr Morgan

Cigar smoke hung in tatters around Juan Vallinova's sombre face. The first light of morning creeping into the stables was silently banishing the night shadows. In the stalls, horses dozed fitfully while the ancient mule was braying loudly. Ever since the Atlanta's rooster had crashed in at the first frost, the mule had taken upon himself the duties of announcing each daybreak at full volume.

Vallinova carefully drew the cigar from between even white teeth and said softly, 'Kill it.'

Adjusting his horse's girth-strap nearby, buck-toothed Slim Whitby blinked owlishly. 'What's that, boss man?'

'The mule. Kill it!'

'Whatever you say, Juan,' Whitby said

reluctantly and, turning from his horse, slowly drew his Colt .45. The animal instantly ceased its racket as though sensing danger. Whitby spun his Colt on his forefinger, playing for time as he glanced over his shoulder at the Mexican. 'Boss . . . ?'

'Kill it . . . if it starts up again.'

Whitby was relieved by the obvious reprieve. He quickly reholstered and returned to his chore. The gangling killer would rather shoot an old grey-headed couple on their way to Sunday service than a mule. Even killers had their soft spots and mules were his.

Dragging on his stogie, Vallinova adjusted the strapping on his left arm. The killer had taken a bullet crease in the clash with Morgan an hour earlier. In the same action, Elroy Dobbs had a finger of his left hand shot away. Yet these were seen as trivial incidents and wouldn't hamper them any.

Action time was drawing closer by the minute. This siege hadn't gone the way Vallinova planned. He'd envisioned the new day revealing Blaze Morgan shot to ribbons and the final victory his for the taking, which was anything but the reality confronting him now.

Looking back as he prepared to mount up, Vallinova saw clearly now that the clash at the tack room had altered the entire outcome of the siege. The girl's attempt to seize the ammunition had taken them unawares, and they had never fully regained the upper hand.

It had seemed they were holding the top cards when Foley had grabbed the girl in the tack room, but then Morgan began blasting his way across to the building in a reckless way nobody had anticipated. The combination of luck and lethal gunplay by Morgan and the youth had resulted in their regaining the house along with its stock of ammunition which Morgan had employed to cut down both Foley Haig and Casey Flynn, slain in one blazing shoot-out.

But now Vallinova was preparing to

do what he knew he should have done at the start. They would go in while they still had the strength and numbers to win.

Vallinova hated to admit mistakes but knew he'd made a serious one in attempting to grind Morgan down instead of rushing the mansion right at the beginning. He'd wanted to minimize his losses, yet here he was now with only two gunmen to back his play after riding into the Atlanta headquarters with a strength of five.

And through all this the great house had stood seemingly aloof and serene, above it all, as it now welcomed the first caress of the sun.

To fire himself up, Vallinova conjured up the days of his youth when he had fought huge bulls for money in the bullrings of Mexico before realizing there was far more profit and excitement in killing men than dumb animals.

The light was strengthening with each moment and birds began chirping in pines and cottonwoods, while the sounds of hoofs and jingling harness seemed magnified in the hushed dawn time.

'Heeyahh!' the killer suddenly yelled, and his horse shot out through the open doors with Whitby and Dobbs hard behind. The racing trio fanned out wide to go charging across the no man's land of the ranch yard behind raging guns.

Riding like a redskin and steering his horse with his knees, Vallinova went storming past the ranch house windows, which exploded in cascades of shimmering glass as his bullets hammered home.

Hard on his heels Whitby and Dobbs worked the levers of their Winchesters with the skill of true professionals against what was as yet but a feeble defence from the mansion.

Vallinova roared triumphantly as he reached the limit of his first sweep, swung his mount around then came charging back.

It was then through the gunsmoke that he first sighted them — three riders dashing down at a gallop from the snow-covered main trail, rifle barrels glittering in the pearly light and long streaks of gunflame leaping out — *towards them!*

With lethal lead flying overhead, understanding came with brutal swiftness to the killer astride the big white horse. For the leading rider wore something upon his vest that glittered in the early light, and as he heeled desperately back the way he had just come, Vallinova realized it was a lawman's star!

For a few bad moments, Vallinova couldn't think, couldn't even guess, how come this nightmare was taking place.

Yet he recovered swiftly. Leaning low over the animal's neck he didn't spare a glance for his henchmen who were still riding in the opposite direction — until they too sighted the danger bearing down upon them at the gallop.

Three riders — looked like lawmen!

From his window above, Blaze Morgan saw the hellions' sudden confusion, made sense of it instantly and shouldered his Winchester straightaway to pump three evenly spaced shots at Vallinova's racing form.

The bullets fell short as the wild-riding Mexican galloped out of range to leave behind him the headlong confrontation between henchmen and city lawmen out in front of the stables.

Sweeping beyond the stables and barn in a wide circle, Vallinova glimpsed Dobbs and Whitby blasting away at the enemy, saw a lawman and his horse go down together at the gallop, the animal screaming in fright before smashing headlong into the stable wall with sickening force.

The surviving rider seemed to falter at that moment, which was all the encouragement Vallinova needed to come storming back without caution or restraint as he galloped directly at the lawmen with his gun held out before him, roaring to his men to back his play.

Momentarily stunned, the badge-toters were slow in reacting. But their weapons jerked up swiftly enough when Vallinova cut loose.

Instantly, Marshal Dolf Carter lurched in his saddle with white-hot death impaling him. He was sliding bloodily to the ground when Vallinova ducked low behind his mount's neck with lead whistling close, then opened up again until forced to reef back violently on the reins to avoid cannoning into a runaway mount.

In the murderous moments that followed all was confusion and chaos beneath a swirling fog of gunsmoke, a breathless stretch of time that saw first Dobbs then Whitby falter before the lawmen's fire. The two were whirling away to retreat when a bullet smacked into Dobbs's mount and the rider went crashing to earth almost under the hoofs of Whitby's mount, causing the rider to rein back violently.

Next moment, St John's Winchester erupted and Whitby slumped across his horse's neck, slipped downwards with one boot caught in the stirrup and was dragged away bouncing violently as the fear-maddened animal bolted through the noise and gunsmoke.

Consumed by a kind of killing trance, Vallinova was unaware of what was happening behind him as he came storming back towards the mansion. He had blunted the lawmen's attack and that was enough for the moment. Rage gripped the killer afresh as the great house loomed closer, and he heard a chanting in his head that said 'Morgan!' over and over, seemingly louder every time.

A face showed at a window above, bringing the rider to a sliding, tail-sitting stop. In that instant, he fired at the window, and Luke Garfield spun away from the broken glass with pain in his shoulder.

Vallinova came out of the saddle in one giant leap that carried him to the porch. With a ferocious grimace, he pushed the door wide and charged inside.

His greeting was a bullet.

Morgan had come racing from the front parlour the moment he'd heard Luke's cry of pain followed by his sister's scream. But such was the killer's incredible speed, he appeared at the end of the passageway just a split second later. Morgan's Colt thundered and a great gout of gunsmoke momentarily engulfed the killer's lithe form.

Vallinova ducked wildly, hurt, but quickly regained his balance to trigger back a thundering reply.

And so they rushed towards the finale of what had begun at the Double Dime Saloon on a rainy night in Yellow Gulch, Oklahoma, when Miguel Vallinova had challenged Blaze Morgan and died in a raging thunderclap of Colts. Here, there were no awed onlookers in a smoke-filled saloon, just two men alone in a dim, high-ceilinged hallway in a great old house that seemed to tremble to its foundations from the thundering roar of that final reckoning with guns and blood.

Suddenly the awful sounds ceased as abruptly as they'd begun.

In the rear room Luke and Hannah Garfield stared at one another, horrified and almost deafened by the gunblasts, seemingly unable to move. A half-mile distant, back on his horse and galloping for the pass on a faltering horse, Slim Whitby heard the voices of the Colts fading now, but didn't even glance back. The final triumph for Vallinova — or the ultimate disaster — whatever it might be, was of no consequence to a hard-hit Whitby now. He would rate this day only as a triumph if he survived — still not realizing he was already a dying man.

Reece and St John had been running for the mansion ever since the sheriff's bullet had cut down Whitby and set him on his doomed course for the pass — which he would never reach. The lawmen had been sprinting while the guns still sounded, but now they slowed, guns at the ready as they stared at the gaping doorway through which Vallinova had disappeared.

It was suddenly deathly quiet.

Abruptly, Reece held up a warning hand to St John and together they checked out the corner. Reece heard footsteps from the hallway and they trained their Colts on the porch, saw a hand appear on the door frame before a dim figure staggered out with gunsmoke still shrouding him.

'Morgan!' Reece gasped.

Morgan heard his name. He saluted with an empty gun then pitched headlong to the floor. Blaze thought he heard Hannah scream, was almost sure it was her hands he could feel attempting to turn him over. Then there was nothing.

* * *

Somehow Marshal Reece wasn't surprised when Morgan showed up for the conference in the great hall next day. He had known Morgan a long time and knew he belonged to an iron breed. He liked the man but nursed the suspicion that he had been lying about Garfield, Greeenberry and the bank money.

'Tough breed that,' Reece murmured to the man at his side as a limping Morgan dropped into a deep chair and busied himself with tobacco and papers, despite the bandages.

'Sure, he's tough enough, I guess. But is he truthful?'

Yesterday Morgan had told the lawmen that Jesse Garfield and Chip Greenberry had been killed by the Vallinova bunch when they'd learned of the bank loot, but which in turn Morgan had eventually recovered. The stolen ten thousand dollars was in the saddle-bags of St John's horse right now, standing saddled and ready for the trail out front.

Reece had known Morgan casually for some time. He knew the man as a respecter of the law yet still sensed he had been lying about Garfield, Greenberry and the bank money.

But then the big question posed itself, 'Did it matter?' — and Reece finally decided that it did not. Garfield and Greenberry had undoubtedly robbed the bank and would have hanged for their crimes in the end. What did it matter how they'd met their fate? Morgan's account certainly didn't seem important enough to be challenged in light of his destruction of the entire Vallinova bunch.

Reece said as much while the sheriff nodded. If the Wichita marshal believed Morgan's story, then that was good enough for Mace St John.

This still left the matter of the bounty money.

They subsequently brought it up only to learn to their astonishment that Morgan was determined to waive all claim on sums payable.

Their puzzlement was understandable, but would not have been so had they been present in Morgan's quarters late the previous night as the wounded gunfighter and his young hosts had convened and made their plans. These involved Morgan staying on to make yet another bid for peace and anonymity for himself here on the Atlanta, while at the same time providing brother and sister with something they seemed never to have really had.

Care and protection.

There was something else Morgan wanted, they were to learn after they'd eventually realized he was serious about rejecting any payment due. His reward, he stated, would be their sworn promise that their reports on events would make no mention of his involvement, that his name was never to be mentioned in relationship to what had happened.

The sheriff couldn't understand, but Marshal Reece seemed to. If Morgan's quest for peaceful obscurity depended upon their silence, then it was an assurance the marshal would readily give. Right now.

He felt the law was getting out of the whole thing cheaply. By contrast, Blaze

Morgan believed if he found what he wanted in this high valley he would have received the richest bounty any gunfighter had ever been paid.

* * *

Morgan waited a full month before writing his letter.

For he had to be sure, and by the end of those winter weeks he knew he was as certain as any man could be. Nobody, either friend or foe, had shown up at Atlanta in that time except Sheriff St John. The lawman had arrived at last with the news that the hearings into the destruction of the Vallinova gang had been finalized without Morgan's name being mentioned.

As far as the law or the world knew, Vallinova and his gang had been wiped out by the peace officers in Weeping Woman Valley, while the return of the ten thousand dollars had closed the books on the Mission Fork bank robbery.

The man reckoned the law was

getting out of the whole thing mighty cheap. But Blaze Morgan believed that if his plan succeeded and he found what he had longed for in the high valley, he would have been lavishly rewarded.

So he penned his letter to Denver, Colorado, and gave it to St John to mail upon his return to Mission Fork.

Then he waited.

The evening winds of a dying winter were knife-sharp up in the Flintlocks. And then it was spring, with new grass peeking through, leaf buds on the trees and migrating birds winging their way home from the warm south.

There was as yet no reply from Denver, and though Blaze Morgan appeared a contented man who worked while his wounds healed, and he settled into his new haven more comfortably with every passing week, he still watched the trail every morning, still hoped.

Then the day came when he rode out to the trail and sighted the sheriff's ancient buckboard coming up from the valleys. St John was at the reins, with a slender, dark-haired figure at his side.

Grace had come!

In the first rush of their reunion she told him of her loneliness without him, her joy on receiving his letter inviting her to join him in this high lonesome. Morgan in return informed her he had given up the gun forever — and had never meant anything more. They chatted like excited children all the way to the mansion and, mooching along behind on Morgan's horse, the sheriff wondered if he had ever been that young.

Wedding plans were well advanced by the time they reached the house and Grace was delighted with everything that met her eye, particularly the great house itself. Of course she realized from his letter that he was merely a tenant here. But surely these could not be his landlords coming out to meet them — these shyly smiling children?

They were indeed, Morgan revealed. But then he had something of far greater magnitude to confess. He intended to adopt Luke and Hannah the moment he and Grace were wed — if she agreed, of course.

It was one hell of a thing to suggest to a bride-to-be, Morgan realized, particularly someone who'd been through what Grace had over the years. Yet the moment after his big announcement, she and Hannah were embracing and he wondered what he'd been worried about.

He was grinning to himself when the sheriff rode up and dismounted stiffly, drawing a folded newspaper from his jacket pocket. He passed it to Morgan without comment. A passage outlined in ink 'confirmed' the rumour that Blaze Morgan the gunfighter had died in Nevada as the result of a gun battle. They even had the name of the man who had killed him.

He smiled broadly as he read his own obituary. Now Blaze Morgan the gunfighter was dead. But Blaze Morgan, the man, would always know his life had begun that day.

We do hope that you have enjoyed reading this large print book.

Did you know that all of our titles are available for purchase?

We publish a wide range of high quality large print books including:
Romances, Mysteries, Classics
General Fiction
Non Fiction and Westerns

Special interest titles available in large print are:
The Little Oxford Dictionary
Music Book, Song Book
Hymn Book, Service Book

Also available from us courtesy of Oxford University Press:
Young Readers' Dictionary
(large print edition)
Young Readers' Thesaurus
(large print edition)

For further information or a free brochure, please contact us at:
Ulverscroft Large Print Books Ltd.,
The Green, Bradgate Road, Anstey,
Leicester, LE7 7FU, England.
Tel: (00 44) 0116 236 4325
Fax: (00 44) 0116 234 0205